W9-BWI-260

*Winner
of the Drue Heinz
Literature Prize
1982*

DANCING
FOR MEN

Robley Wilson, Jr.

MIDDLEBURY COLLEGE LIBRARY

University of Pittsburgh Press

PS
3573
.I4665
D3

3/1983
am. Lit.

Published by the University of Pittsburgh Press,
Pittsburgh, Pa. 15260
Copyright © 1983 by Robley Wilson, Jr.
All rights reserved
Feffer and Simons, Inc., London
Manufactured in the United States of America

Library of Congress Cataloging in Publication Data

Wilson, Robley.
   Dancing for men.

   I. Title.
PS3573.I4665D3   813'.54   82-2602
ISBN 0-8229-3466-3   AACR2

Some of these stories have appeared (often in slightly different form or under a different title) in the following periodicals: *Antaeus* ("A Fear of Children" and "Land Fishers"); *The Cresset* ("War Games, 1952"); *Fiction International* ("Thief"); *Minnesota Review* ("Mothers" and "A Story with Sex and Violence"); *Mississippi Review* ("Children," "Crossings," and "Fashion"); *Northern Ohio Live* ("Artists and Their Models"); *Pieces* ("The Hundred Steps"); *Story Quarterly* ("Wasps").

Contents

Dancing for Men

Despair

THE first three years of his marriage he could scarcely credit his good fortune; he loved Laura, delighted in being seen with her (she was "a gem," as his mother had said even before the engagement), and when they went to bed together he thought he had never known such pleasure, such excitement, and that one night when the two of them were making love the joy would be so much more than he could bear that his heart would simply stop. Then he would go through Eternity just as he had died—naked and erect and with all his millions of nerve ends chafed into a state bordering on Paradise.

The next three years were not so remarkable, but the marriage seemed to him certainly as good as most he knew about. In those years Laura had suffered through two miscarriages and a bout with bronchial pneumonia, and what with those misfortunes and her dogged refusal to stop smoking she grew thinner—pale and smelling of tobacco, a woman whose visible unhappiness made him unsure of himself. It was as if the gem his mother had discerned had fallen out of its setting and left a gold-clawed hollowness. In bed she was much changed; the failed pregnancies had seemed to turn her against lovemaking. It occurred to him that in his fantasies of the Hereafter there was no sign of Laura, and that perhaps his real destiny was to die alone.

Now, after ten years of marriage going on eleven, he imagined himself a martyr. Lately Laura had taken up politics as

3

though that was a true vocation whose call she had heard but failed to understand through most of her life with him. "I was preoccupied with you," she told him one night when she came home from a precinct meeting after neglecting to leave either a note on the table or supper in the microwave. "There are more important things in my life than cooking and trying to keep up with your mooning about."

"How much trouble is it to make a casserole?" he wanted to know. "How hard is it to put something in the refrigerator for a hungry man who's worked hard all day trying to sell American cars to people who'd rather buy Jap?"

"More than I have time for," she said. "And Edith Martin tells me nobody at the showroom is wearing themselves out. How much trouble is it for *you* to make a casserole?"

Sometimes, evenings in front of the television, he wondered what his life might be like if he had been born a hundred years ago. Not that he wouldn't miss television, but the idea of being married to an old-fashioned woman, more like his mother—who'd had no ambitions of her own—appealed to him. That had been, he barely remembered, one of Laura's supposed charms. He had brought home a succession of girlfriends when he was just back from the tour of army duty which had taken him no nearer Vietnam than Oakland, California. ("I'm playing the field," he told his father at the airport homecoming. "Life's too short to be serious about women." He had felt that, strongly; at Oakland he had seen the boxed and bagged corpses of hundreds of men no older than himself.) Laura had been the first of the field, and though he showed off at least a half-dozen after her, it was Laura his father liked best.

"She's the honey of the bunch," he told his son, "just as sweet as your mother was when we took up together after the war"—meaning World War Two. "Shy, aims to please, all eyes for you. If she can cook, you better grab her."

Today he would tell his father—except the man had been dead for three years—sure, she *can* cook, but she won't. She had involved herself in the E.R.A. when it looked as if some of the states who'd voted for it might have a change of heart, and she spent nights in the church basement addressing envelopes that sowed the argument of women's rights across the plains and prairies. When the abortion issue crested, Laura rode with it, drawing on the wisdom of her miscarriages and preaching the right of a woman to be "landlady of her own bodily house." Recently she had gone over to the Democrats, stuffing and sealing and mailing, and even making speeches whose rhetoric she often practiced on her husband.

"You ought not to talk like that about a man who's going to be the President," he would say.

Sometimes at work, where things were slow and getting slower, he would daydream about a wife who was, say, Oriental—Vietnamese, perhaps (he'd heard stories about them from men who came back alive), or, better, Japanese (stories from his father, God rest him). It was bad enough for those tiny people to make the kind of automobile Americans seemed to want—and so his take-home week by week got more anemic—without their also having the kind of marriage he coveted. He knew all about those Jap women: their bow and lick and *yes, husband,* their flimsy kimonos, black hair pinned high. *Shy, aims to please, all eyes for you.*

Laura had let him down—it was as if she had revealed her true self bit by bit, the way auto companies introduced new models by showing the outline under a sheet and then slowly unveiling all the chrome and jeweled paintwork. No children. No understanding. No respect. He remembered when he was twelve and his parents owned the house on the outskirts of Omaha, one day he had ridden his pony—that chunky, stubborn Welsh—home from the boarding stables. The pony had dropped a load in front of Joey Miller's driveway, down at the end of the street, and before he was allowed to ride back to the stables his mother commanded him to clean it up.

"It's your horse," she said. "You just fetch the shovel and spread that good manure in the garden out back."

And so he had—had walked to the Millers', lugging the shovel; had loaded it up with the dark dung still steaming and pungent; had started toward home holding the ripe burden as far out ahead of him as he could. Joey's dad was washing the car in the driveway, had watched the whole process of his cleaning the paved street. "Hey there, young man," he hollered, "you gonna eat that?"

Humiliation. How could a grownup do that to a boy? He had walked straight on, ears and cheeks flaming; he had hurled the dung into the garden with all the force behind it of his hatred for adults. *For his mother.* If he did not carry the grudge, he carried the memory like a stench endlessly in his nostrils.

On the day of the elections, at breakfast, Laura said: "I imagine you're determined to vote for that movie star of yours."

"Oh," he said, "is today the day?"

"You ought to think about it. Really. What it means to us women; businessmen getting fatter; generals spending welfare money."

He sipped his coffee. "It sounds like stuff I can live with," he said. "I'm not so well off as I was four years ago. Neither are you."

"That's you," she said. She gestured with a cigarette she had just lit. "Look out for number one."

"Maybe we should just skip voting," he said. "We're only going to cancel each other out. I won't if you won't."

She looked at him as if she had heard a story not to be believed. "I'll be poll-watching at Kennedy Grade School," she said. "You'll have to fend for yourself for lunch."

He drove to Martin Motors wondering at his clumsiness. In the back of his mind had lurked the notion that Laura could be deceived—that he might persuade her not to vote, would promise the same, then he would sneak out to the polls just before they closed. Even if she knew, it would be too late for her to do anything about it. Had he really thought that? But matters were desperate. Surely the Republicans would put the Japs in their place, stop the imports—save him from the embarrassment of never having any spending money.

At work he phoned his "prospects"—mere habit; seldom nowadays did anything come of the ritual—and sat at his desk in the furthest corner of the showroom reading *Forbes* magazine. Around eleven o'clock he heard odd noises and strolled out to the repair shop to see what was going on. At the back, off to the right of the parts window, three of his fellow salesmen and one of the mechanics had made a target with a felt marker on the side of one of the several cartons of paper towels stored there. Harold Simms had a .22 target pistol; the four of them had been taking turns firing at the crude bull's-eye. He could picture what the towels inside were going to look like, but when he was invited to shoot, he accepted. It was the first time he had fired any weapon since basic training almost fifteen years ago; the pistol felt foreign in his hand, and he missed the center of the target by at least a foot.

When he went home for lunch he found in the refrigerator some thin slices of pastrami and one slice of American cheese wrapped in cellophane. He made a pastrami and cheese sandwich and sat in the living room with the day's newspaper, eating slowly because the bread wasn't thawed. Then, since the target shoot had been the greatest event of his morning and there seemed no percentage in going back to work, he went down to the basement refrigerator and got out a beer. He phoned the showroom and told Harold Simms he was taking half of one of his vacation days.

At four he voted. He voted straight Republican, except for one Democratic state senator he had once sold a car to, and voted *yes* to all of the judges listed on the voting machine even though he had never heard of any of them. When he came to the state E.R.A. amendment he pushed down the *no* lever without a thought; it seemed precisely the right choice, given the condition of the country, his marriage, his day. What Laura didn't comprehend was that all elections were no more sensible than his first job hunt after the army discharged him, when he had stood in line in the hallway of an insurance company headquarters in Des Moines and a man in shirtsleeves had walked down the line of applicants pointing at random, saying: "I'll see you—and you—and you," until out of sixteen of them five had been chosen. *And none of them me.*

That night in bed he tried to tell Laura what was wrong with his work, his country, himself. He told her how he thought he deserved better, how he could not understand why he had never risen in the world. He told her how he had gone on believing in the *rightness* of Vietnam even after a year of copying information off the shipping tags of dead soldiers onto the forms that would go home to the parents to rub their noses in grief, how you had to realize the threat of those undersized, expressionless people who wanted by sheer numbers to smother the rest of the world. He told her he would never get over the way he had been treated by some of his old friends at the high school reunion he had taken her to, the way they had acted as if he was a criminal and the way they refused to notice that he had never left the U.S. He told her his day: the pointless phone calls, the target-shooting in the shop with some of the mechanics joking about the sanity of salesmen who had nothing to do but look at girlie magazines and be jerk-offs. He told her he had voted flat against the g.d. E.R.A. amendment, but it hadn't made him feel any better.

"I don't know what to do," he said. "I really don't."

"Do you want to quit Martin?"

"Maybe. But I don't know where I'd go for another job."

She studied him as if she were concerned. The lamp on the bedside table was lighted and it cast a glow across half her face, a soft shadow on the other half. He could see, like a pleasure renewed, how she had looked when his father had been dazzled by her, and he thought that if she could make herself quit smoking he might want her more.

"I don't," he said. "There's just no work lying around," and he reminded her again about the roulette of his first job search in Des Moines. "Times were a lot better then, too," he said.

She shook her head. "That was the year they killed six children because the men in government were afraid to have peace."

"I mean the job situation was better," he said.

Then she did a surprising thing. She took one of his hands in both of hers and drew it to her lips and kissed his knuckles, and all at once she was weeping as he had not seen her weep since the loss of the second baby.

"No," she said. "Nothing is better," and she lay against him, her shoulders shaking, her rare tears wet on his face. He embraced the slight weight of her; he thought he understood how worn out she was from all the election work and the disappointment of having failed at something she believed in.

Dancing for Men

WHEN she was fifteen, Sarah Meredith went twice to a traveling carnival with David Willard.

The first time was the result of negotiations with her mother over names and hours and allowance. The wealth of David's parents—his father was a GM executive—was the most persuasive of her bargaining counters. Money spoke loudly and firmly to Mrs. Meredith; it transformed ordinary young men into "nice boys," and in the instance at hand made David nearly a saint. Except for the Willard money, Sarah knew she would likely as not have been obliged to stay home. Two years earlier it had required days and days of tears and fist-pounding before her mother—largely at the urging of her father, who tended to spoil her and whose tolerance for "scenes" was less than his wife's—gave in and let her accept her high school's invitation to become a cheerleader. The argument against cheerleading had to do with the "get-up"; it showed too much leg, was flimsy and indecent, would incite even nice boys to God-knew-what excesses. In general—it seemed to Sarah at that age—her mother was so opposed and alert to the fact of sex as to make the daughter wonder how her parents had managed her own existence. The thought amused her all the more, the more she learned about sexuality. Perhaps her mother was like Edris, who had pretended to fall asleep in the back of Tommy Kubichek's car and didn't pretend to wake up until after he had undressed her and really begun to hurt her. It was a mystery—this continual discrepancy between what one did and what one *ought* to be doing.

11

She'd had no idea what to expect from David. She had never gone out with him, not even to a movie, but she was aware of him—at football and basketball games, for instance, where he always managed to sit in the bleacher section that was her cheerleading responsibility—and she had held him in the back of her mind, *in reserve*, against some day when his niceness and his money might be useful to her. She did not think she was attracted to him, though there had been times when she sought him out in preference to some one of her girl friends—for his calmness, usually, his downright reluctance to talk or, when he did talk, to raise his voice above the barely audible. She believed that David was one of those boys who like to *worship from afar*, to be a *secret admirer;* she rather thought he liked suffering—or the idea of suffering. She did not think she was influenced by his—his parents'—money, or by the fancy house he lived in, or even by his being a junior and thus more than a year older than she was. Always her mind turned back to his steadiness, his reliability, his splendid unwillingness to upset the world around him. He was tall for his age, or at least taller than most of the boys in his class, and awkward-looking, thin and long-boned. As if self-conscious about his height he walked with a slouch; when he stood still he supported himself on one leg, the other seeming to be wrapped around its mate. *Stork.* David was, all in all, unthreatening.

Which was important. If her parents with their uneasiness about the mere abstraction of boys had not limited her dating career, Sarah would have restricted herself almost as severely. Something about them—boys—disturbed her in a fashion having as much to do with aesthetics as with anything else. What was wrong with them? Their clothes never fit them—they were all bony wrists and strips of ugly socks—and they seemed to have only rough edges. Either they were shaggy because they needed haircuts, or they looked like skinned poodles because they'd just gotten one; their faces were a mess—blotched and pocked, or showing little sprouts of beard and mustache that might better be chopped away. They had no manners, no sense of what manners *were*. They moved down the halls of the high school like unbridled ponies, lumbering into anyone approaching them, whinnying with coarse laughter, pushing and bucking against one another; they frightened her with their self-centered ways. And most of them smelled peculiar. Sweat, was it, from the gym classes they pretended to despise but secretly loved for the liberation of *romping?* After-shave, to show off with? Or was it some sheer animal odor she could not name? One of the differences between girls and boys—she had thought about this quite seriously—was that girls existed within bounds, but boys spilled out all over, as if they didn't know about their limitations. It was a distinction that made girls seem safer.

Probably David was somewhere between safety and risk. It often seemed to Sarah that his eyes were always on her—especially at the basketball games, when it looked as if his body was trying to imitate her movements but was restrained by the presence of other spectators around him. He was not only better dressed than other boys, but appeared smoother-edged, more carefully made. She did not feel that if she collided with him in the halls she would bruise; instead there would be only a tender place, quickly fading. She had no hesitation about proposing that he take her to the carnival, and in his reserved way he had agreed.

"I've already been, you know, but I suppose I could go again."

"Was it fun?"

"Oh, sure. We had a good time."

She did not ask questions about the carnival itself; she could imagine what it was like—tacky and dirty, the carnival people speaking their own language and cheating everyone who could not speak it: there would be shooting galleries with rifles misaimed, milk bottle throws whose bottles were so weighted you could never knock them over, freak shows in which the freaks were fake, weight guessers whose scales were dishonestly calibrated. All she knew was that she desperately wanted to see for herself.

When he called for her on a Friday night she had dressed up for him—blouse and skirt, instead of the jeans her mother had suggested might be more appropriate for "that dirty, smelly circus," and a bright green ribbon in her hair. David wore the same clothes she had seen him wear at school that day.

"I hope you don't mind walking," he said. "Mom's car's in the shop. I tried to get Dad's, but he and Mom are going out to Ann Arbor to visit some friends."

"I didn't know you had your license," Sarah said.

"Are you kidding? I've had it almost two years."

"I don't mind walking," she said. "Really."

This was in May. Many days—like this one—were summery, cooling down only later in the evening when the sun was long set and the wind came up. Sarah had brought along a sweater, David wore a thin jacket. She would remember the walk as pleasant, friendly. David didn't make her self-conscious because she was younger—didn't treat her as an inferior, didn't pretend she was a possession he was trying out, the way one or two other upperclassmen had when she worked with them on the school play. It offended her to be thought of as *young*. If David had reached over and held her hand as they walked, she would not have been angry—surprised, yes—but would have understood the gesture to be a confirmation of her maturity. They did not touch at all, in fact; they were two schoolmates on their way to the carnival, not a couple on a date.

And what had they done there? They had watched the shell-game man—a gaunt, deft-fingered character with a foreign accent who manipulated the walnut shells with his hands and the onlookers with his spiel. They had gone to a shooting gallery, where David despite his money had won nothing. They rode the bump-em cars—three times over, because careering and jolting into other people was as much fun as Sarah ever remembered having—until David confessed that his neck hurt.

"I'll sue you for whiplash," he threatened.

Then they had roamed through the freak shows—the display of fetuses in a progression of glass jars; the thin man, so emaciated she thought certainly he was almost dead; the ugly and sickening wild boy. The bearded lady had seemed to her to be authentic; the hermaphrodite—she didn't know about that sort of confusion, though she had read articles about sex-change operations.

"I've never been to anything like this," she told David. "Mother would have a stroke."

"Over a carnival?" He marveled. "You lead a sheltered life."

"I truly think I do," she said.

"That's what you ought to see." He had pointed to a tent fronted by a stage and a bulb-lit sign: *MELITA*. A barker had gathered a crowd—all of them men—and was beginning to sell tickets to whatever was going on inside. Above his head was an enormous, garish painting of a half-naked woman with huge breasts and hips.

"Why ought I to see that?"

He acted embarrassed. "A different education," he said. "Forget it."

"What kind of education? Sex?"

"Really—forget it."

"Let's go in."

"I could go in. Not you."

"Why not?"

"Girls aren't allowed. Women aren't."

"Why? What happens?"

"Oh—" He moved his hands awkwardly, helplessly.

"Is it dirty? Something obscene?"

"Never mind," he said.

"Why so *cute*, David?" She stopped walking, obliging him to stop. "Am I too damned young?"

"No. Listen, she just dances."

"Is she a strip-teaser? I mean does she take her clothes off while you watch her?"

"She just comes out that way—nude—and dances."

"Then let's go see her."

"I told you, Sarah. They won't let girls in."

"Who would stop me?"

"The police, that's who."

"Seriously?"

"Seriously. There's a cop inside the tent with the crowd."

There seemed nothing further to be said; yet to be prevented from going where David was permitted to go, seeing what he could see, undercut the evening for her.

"I think probably we should leave, David," she told him.

"All right," he said. "It's a nice night just to walk."

"But I want you to take me to see that woman dance."

"I told you," David said, "they won't let you in."

"I'll dress like a boy. They won't know."

He looked at her, sidelong. They had turned onto Dearborn Street; her house was less than a half block away.

"God, Sarah—it's a pretty raunchy dance."

"I'm sure I've seen worse," she said.

"Where?"

"You know those playing cards Darryl Jenks carries around with him?"

David's eyes widened in horror. "He showed you those? Oh, *Sarah*." He fell silent.

What was it? She imagined Darryl must have broken the rules by showing her pictures of what the two sexes might do together—that it was perfectly all right for a boy to savage a girl *in fact* (as Tommy had savaged Edris in the car), but not in the abstract.

In the end David agreed. All he had to do, Sarah told him, was to bring a cap with him when he picked her up the following evening after supper. She told her parents she was going to the movies; her mother rejoiced that her daughter was going out a second time with such a nice young man—*nice* meaning that the young man was not likely to lead her across the border between sexes.

In the afternoon Sarah practiced walking. That, she felt, was the most difficult of the temporary manly arts she had to carry off, and she went about house and yard in an exaggerated swagger, flat-footed, as graceless as she could manage, tucking her closed fingers into the back pockets of her Levi's. She had determined that she needed to do very little to herself cosmetically; at fifteen she was still small-breasted, and she had inherited her mother's slim hips. Her *costume* consisted of tennis shoes and white socks, the Levi's, a blue work shirt she borrowed from her father, and a zippered windbreaker. As a precaution only, she wore under the shirt a summer tube top whose elastic had already been uncomfortably tight last year. She saw to it that the tennis shoes were scruffy, that the socks drooped. She scrubbed her face and put on no makeup.

David arrived on foot, his parents' cars again unavailable, so she had the distance to the carnival grounds to practice her masculine walk—the odd swagger that made her feel like a round-bottomed doll no degree of pushing could quite knock over.

"What do you think?" she asked at the end of the second block.

"About what?"

"The way I walk. Do I look like a boy?"

"Sarah, I can't tell." He seemed genuinely perplexed. "I know who you are; I can't pretend you're something else."

"Let me have the cap."

He took off his cap and gave it to her. "It's supposed to be a Greek fisherman's hat," he said. "My mom bought it for me in Athens."

"Really?" She piled her hair on top of her head and froze it there with two amber combs she had borrowed from the silver box on her mother's dressing table. Then she put on the cap, pushing stray wisps up under the sweatband. She fussed with the bill. "How's this?"

"A little more forward—down over your eyes."

"Like so?"

"That's better."

She nudged him with an elbow. "Okay, Davey, let's go scope out that Melita broad."

David looked pained. "Cute," he said.

"David? Don't be upset. Nobody's going to say anything."

And nobody did. David bought the tickets, and he and Sarah were carried along the short canvas corridor into the tent's interior by a tide of men—most of them older: thirties, forties, she thought. She felt very small, very much a child among grownups.

"We have to get somewhere near the front," she whispered, "or else I'm not going to see a thing over all these dirty old men."

"Just shove on through."

She managed to elbow a path to the front of the crowd and found herself against a stage, a four-foot-high platform lighted from the back of the tent by a floodlight. A yellowish-gray curtain—perhaps it was white but soiled—hung from a line at the rear of the stage and extended to both sides of the tent. To the left, at the edge of the stage, was a portable phonograph, its power cord trailing over the rim of the platform. When she tried to look about her, she couldn't see much; men towered over her.

"How many do you suppose are in here?" she asked David.

He stood on tiptoe and looked back. "Fifty or sixty," he said.

"That's fifty or sixty dollars. How many times does she do this?"

"I don't know. The show only lasts about ten minutes."

"Say they do three shows an hour," she said. "That's almost two hundred dollars."

David nodded.

"Could it be more than that?"

"You'll see," David said.

Someone put a scratchy record on the phonograph and she began to see. At first she was disappointed, for when Melita appeared through a slit in the back curtain—though she was a youngish woman with a pretty face, and Sarah felt an instant attraction to the dancer—she was dressed almost respectably. She wore a harem costume, the top made of gauzy material with sleeves slit to expose the skin, the pantaloons of a glossy, satiny fabric that reached below her knees. A silver vest covered her bosom; she wore several bracelets on each wrist and a single gold-colored bangle on her left ankle. When Melita danced, she clanked. *What is it?* Sarah thought; *what draws them to her?* Yet when the woman moved into the dance, the dark coins of her nipples showed through the sheer blouse under the moving panels of the vest, and when the bending of Melita's knees opened the sides of the pantaloons, no trace of bikini or g-string showed. When she turned away from the men and slowly lay back, arms outward for balance, her eyes were closed. She was so supple, her hair brushed the stage floor before she finally lifted her arms and raised herself again. the men murmured among themselves; a few applauded; one man reached out as if he intended to touch the woman, but she danced—eyes open now—lightly away from him.

"This is about as sexy as Bible school," Sarah whispered.

"Wait," David said.

Abruptly the dance ended. The tent held a brief ripple of applause; the dancer bowed and disappeared behind the dingy curtain.

"That's it? I thought you said she was naked."

"I said to *wait*." He was angry; she wondered why.

She waited. She felt that the men were more impatient than she was, and that David's anger was, really, his own kind of impatience. Something else was supposed to happen, and it frustrated her that she was the only person around here not to know *what*. She didn't dare ask David again. Everywhere she heard cigarette lighters clicking, smelled tobacco smoke, felt a gradual rising in the level of talk, in the instances of coarse laughter, in the weight of anticipation. No one was leaving. She glanced shyly at David; his teeth seemed to be gritted, and the muscles in his jaw were working nervously; he looked straight ahead.

Then the barker appeared onstage from behind the curtain.

Scattered clapping greeted him, and he waved to the men in the crowd the way one acknowledges old friends. "Gentlemen," he said, as if he were beginning a speech. The crowd hooted at the word; the barker lifted his palms for silence. "I call you *gentlemen*," he said, "because the law is here tonight"—he gestured in the direction of the uniformed policeman standing at the rear of the tent—"and I've been duly warned not to call a spade a spade, or to otherwise use any honest words that might offend all you lecherous bastards." The men laughed approval, whooped and whistled. "Now I see a few familiar faces in this company of saints, so I don't have to tell you that the beauteous Melita, behind this curtain—"

"That's the truth," said a voice. "All of us thinks Melita's behind is a beaut!" The crowd jeered.

"—is real eager to let you gentlemen, not to forget you lecherous bastards as well, have another look-see at her wares. And I don't have to tell you more than once that the tariff for this second show is two American dollars and that it begins just as soon as all you are inside and ready—and please, men, nobody under the age of eighteen years." The barker moved to the side of the stage and jumped to the ground; the men surged toward the curtain at that side of the tent.

"Two dollars more!" she said into David's ear.

"Don't you have enough?"

"Could you let me have a dollar?"

He reached into his shirt pocket and unfolded a thin packet of bills. "Here."

She took the dollar from him. "Thank you," she said, "but I don't think he'll let us pass."

"Why not?"

"Under age."

David grinned at her. "Don't worry," he said. "They have to say that."

But Sarah fretted. She knew how young she looked as a girl; as a boy she would seem no more than a ten-year-old to anyone who seriously studied her—never mind the cap bill, and never mind the big-kid swagger. When she drew even with the barker and held out the two dollars she saw the hesitation in the way his hand reached for the money. Peering at him from the shadow of the fisherman's hat she saw his eyes—cold and gray—narrow to read the details of her child's face. Then he took the money. "Got to start sometime. Right, son?" And already his attention was behind her and she was on the other side of the forbidden curtain.

David nudged her. "I told you so," he said.

When Melita appeared the second time she seemed to Sarah incredibly pale—so white as to seem bloodless—and for the first few moments the dancer's movements were ghostlike. It was this *apparition* of Melita she would always remember, and not only the excitement of being taken into an alien world with its sweet, mildew smell of rotted grasses, the good-natured jostling, the odor—as real on these men as on the boys at school—of something especially and mysteriously male. *If you'd been watching too brilliant an image, and then closed your eyes:* that was how she would recall the woman on the stage—something burnt onto the screen of sight, so that she saw it imposed over the commonplace objects of the present world. Though it might have been the lights. When she looked up she saw two flood-lights aimed toward the stage, and over each of them a pale violet gel—so the light *appeared* white but was really tinted. Whatever it was, it accented the woman's lips, her fingernails and toenails—all so red they seemed black.

But Melita was naked, as David had promised her. Only the bangle at her left ankle—a small golden disc suspended from a thin chain—had survived from the earlier costume.

"She's totally nude," Sarah whispered.

"I *told* you."

"Do you think the man at the entrance knew I was a girl?"

"Probably."

"Why did he let me in? Just for the two dollars?"

"For God's sake, Sarah—" Her name was a hiss.

Melita had walked to the front of the stage, her arms outspread—her face, so far as Sarah could read it, absolutely expressionless. Gaze straight ahead, apparently above the audience; mouth set, chin high and a little pushed forward.

"She truly is beautiful," Sarah whispered.

And so she thought. Melita's skin was unblemished, and she was shapely without being plump—slender-waisted, wrists and ankles almost skinny—though she was older than Sarah had first guessed, perhaps in her late twenties. Only a touch of shadow under the eyes, little sardonic lines at the corners of her mouth. If Melita had flaws, the light was too bright to shade or contrast them. Her breasts were round but high—*they say when you can hold a pencil under them, they're sagging*—the nipples surprisingly larger and darker than her own, the belly unscarred and with a deep navel; under the belly— *Oh.* Under the belly, no hair. Melita had shaved the pubic hair; the outer vaginal lips were a ruddy pink between her thighs, looking like—like something odd, *like a dried apricot.*

"She shaves between her legs," Sarah whispered. She touched David's arm; his muscles were tense.

"Yes," he said.

I wonder why. But Melita was beginning her dance—though this was less a real dance than something very much like the floor exercises of a gymnast—a way of showing off the body's litheness, part by part; a stepping and flexing of the legs, a milling and reaching of the arms, a display of the torso's strength. The men clapped hands, they talked to her, some of them whistled. She did a somersault, a graceful cartwheel; she came to an effortless handstand and walked across the stage on her palms. Finally she brought all motion to a halt in a kneeling position at the front of the stage, her thighs slightly apart, her hands on the stage floor, her head bowed so the dark hair flowed down between her knees. The men applauded and chattered approvingly among themselves. Sarah tugged at David's arm.

"Is that all she does?" she said into his ear.

He shook free. He refused to look at her; she could tell his teeth were gritted.

But if she talked too much it was because she didn't know what was supposed to happen in this new world, and it was because she was so close to Melita—in the front row, the best vantage in the house—that she wished for the dance to go on and on. She had never been so intimate with an entertainer; when Melita lifted her head Sarah could see the beads of sweat on her forehead, between her breasts, on her thighs. She knew Melita's effort from the way she breathed, the way she held her mouth. She could see that Melita was clenching and unclenching her fists, even as the men clapped for her. She could even read what was engraved on the gold disc at Melita's ankle: *Love Jesus*—in italics with tiny decorative serifs on the *L* and the *J*. Sarah wanted to nudge David again, to tell him what the anklet said, but she thought better of it. She would remember to tell him later. *Love Jesus*. The words disturbed her in this place.

Still on her knees, Melita had begun a different performance, stroking herself, sliding her hands along the backs of her legs to the bend of the knees, caressing the insides of her thighs and letting her hands meet over her belly, rubbing her breasts—the fingers lingering at the nipples—traveling her hands over her shoulders, behind her head; now she bowed and let the hands pull her black hair forward before they dropped again to the floor beside her. *Clenching her fists*. The men were hooting and shouting, and Melita threw her head back to toss the long hair into place; she looked to be smiling, but Sarah was near enough to see—from the way she showed her teeth, from the curl of the lips—how much the smile was like an animal's snarl. David, too, was applauding. He leaned into Sarah.

"I think that's so sexy," he said. Melita had begun to repeat the caressing of herself, and he watched her intently—eyes bright, mouth open. "She really turns a guy on."

Sarah thought that was probably true. It interested her that the reflected light from Melita's white body played on David's face and made shadows; it interested her that he so much liked actions the dancer despised. "Maybe,"she said.

Maybe. Sarah supposed that what excited David was the idea that the hands playing over Melita's body were *his* hands— that was what was intended, what the audience was to imagine—but this was not subtle; this was gross. *Sexy?* Now Melita was fondling herself at the crotch, legs opened, her dark-nailed fingers rubbing the slit of her sex. The men liked that; Sarah could feel the weight of them, the heat of them, crushing her against the stage. She was feeling queasy—the smoke, the closeness, sights she wished she could turn away from. How could you love Jesus and do such things?

"How's about a smoke, Melita?" The voice was at Sarah's left; she couldn't see who had spoken.

"Time for a cigarette, babe?" A different man.

David poked her. "Watch this. It's amazing."

"What?" she said. "What's happening?"

"Watch and see."

"Here you go, Melita." A man behind David reached over him to the stage, offering a lighted cigarette. The dancer took it, held it above her head so all could see it, then did a graceful pirouette to the center of the stage.

The two floodlights went out. In their place the beam of an unfiltered spotlight cut through the smokiness of the tent. Melita took a puff on the cigarette; its tip glowed bright orange and—as if that small point of color were a signal—the men were silent.

"Watch," David said.

Sarah watched. There was no music to soften the sharp edges of this performance, no pink gels to highlight it, no applause or whistles or cheers. An uneasy quiet—a cough, the clearing of a throat, nervous whispers, the sound close by her of men breathing as if they had been climbing or running—settled in the darkened tent; the path of light was a cylinder filled with swirls of smoke. Melita stood in the center of the light, her hips moving suggestively, her head back, the hand holding the cigarette falling slowly lower—to the level of her shoulders, her breasts, her stomach—until it stopped below her belly. As her hand dropped, the light grew smaller; now it was a circle scarcely a foot in diameter, illuminating her thighs, her shaved mound, the burning cigarette in her right hand. Sarah put her own hand to her mouth. She knew what was going to happen.

With practiced slowness Melita brought the cigarette between her legs—her knees parted and bent, so that the intimacy, the near relationship of her body with its admirers, was closer still—and separating the petals of her sex with the fingers of her left hand inserted the end of the cigarette with her right. She took away her hands; the cigarette remained. Then, even though Melita seemed to do nothing, Sarah saw the tip of the cigarette glow orange. In the tent: no one talking, no one moving. *This is horrid.* Now Melita removed the cigarette and held it at arm's length. A half-dozen hands reached out; she gave the cigarette into one of them. The spotlight was unwavering, fixed between her thighs. With an abrupt forward thrust of her pelvis—it happened together with a sound she made, as if the action required great physical effort—a puff of gray smoke expelled itself from her sex and drifted over the audience in the shape of an imperfect circle.

Melita sank to her knees and sat back on her heels, the spotlight enlarging to bathe all of her. She spread her arms and bowed her head into the whoops and laughter and clapping of the men. *Not showing her face.* Sarah turned and bumped against David; she pushed at him. She wanted to run away, but she was afraid if she opened her mouth to say so she would be sick in front of them all. So she pushed dumbly at David, trying to steer him through the crowd and out through the flap of the tent.

"What's the matter?" David pushed back, to maintain his balance. "Wasn't that something?"

She shook her head and shoved harder. The barker had resumed the stage and was making some new announcement—*my God, is there another curtain, another horror?*—but she couldn't force her mind to take it in. At last David got the idea and began to work his way out, opening a path for her. Outdoors in the cool dusk she ran to the side of the tent furthest from the lighted midway and took her hand away from her mouth; she did not get sick, but her stomach was churning as if she ought to, and her throat held a harsh, sour taste. She could feel cold sweat on her face and under her clothing. David stood beside her, looking at her. She took off the fisherman's cap and gave it to him, pulled out the combs and let her hair flow. She felt better, though if she closed her eyes she could see *that ugly apricot* pouting open to discharge its dirty smoke ring, and she knew that somehow, some way, she was going to come apart during the walk home with David, and he would have no idea what was wrong with her.

Thief

HE is waiting at the airline ticket counter when he first
notices the young woman. She has glossy black hair
pulled tightly into a knot at the back of her head—the man imagines it loosed and cascading to the small of her back—and carries
over the shoulder of her leather coat a heavy black purse. She
wears black boots of soft leather. He struggles to see her face—
she is ahead of him in line—but it is not until she has bought her
ticket and turns to walk away that he realizes her beauty, which
is pale and dark-eyed and full-mouthed, and which quickens his
heartbeat. She seems aware that he is staring at her and lowers
her gaze abruptly.

The airline clerk interrupts. The man gives up looking at the
woman—he thinks she may be about twenty-five—and buys a
round-trip, coach class ticket to an eastern city.

His flight leaves in an hour. To kill time, the man steps into
one of the airport cocktail bars and orders a scotch and water.
While he sips it he watches the flow of travelers through the
terminal—including a remarkable number, he thinks, of un-
attached pretty women dressed in fashion magazine clothes—
until he catches sight of the black-haired girl in the leather coat.
She is standing near a Travelers Aid counter, deep in conversation with a second girl, a blonde in a cloth coat trimmed with
gray fur. He wants somehow to attract the brunette's attention,
to invite her to have a drink with him before her own flight
leaves for wherever she is traveling, but even though he be-

lieves for a moment she is looking his way he cannot catch her eye from out of the shadows of the bar. In another instant the two women separate; neither of their directions is toward him. He orders a second scotch and water.

When next he sees her he is buying a magazine to read during the flight and becomes aware that someone is jostling him. At first he is startled that anyone would be so close as to touch him, but when he sees who it is he musters a smile.

"Busy place," he says.

She looks up at him—Is she blushing?—and an odd grimace crosses her mouth and vanishes. She moves away from him and joins the crowds in the terminal.

The man is at the counter with his magazine, but when he reaches into his back pocket for his wallet the pocket is empty. *Where could I have lost it?* he thinks. His mind begins enumerating the credit cards, the currency, the membership and identification cards; his stomach churns with something very like fear. *The girl who was so near to me*, he thinks—and all at once he understands that she has picked his pocket.

What is he to do? He still has his ticket, safely tucked inside his suitcoat—he reaches into the jacket to feel the envelope, to make sure. He can take the flight, call someone to pick him up at his destination—since he cannot even afford bus fare—conduct his business and fly home. But in the meantime he will have to do something about the lost credit cards—call home, have his wife get the numbers out of the top desk drawer, phone the card companies—so difficult a process, the whole thing suffocating. What shall he do?

First: Find a policeman, tell what has happened, describe the young woman; damn her, he thinks, for seeming to be attentive to him, to let herself stand so close to him, to blush prettily when he spoke—and all the time she wanted only to steal from him. And her blush was not shyness but the anxiety of being caught; that was most disturbing of all. *Damned deceitful creatures.* He will spare the policeman the details—just tell what she has done, what is in the wallet. He grits his teeth. He will probably never see his wallet again.

He is trying to decide if he should save time by talking to a guard near the X-ray machines when he is appalled—and elated—to see the black-haired girl. (*Ebony-Tressed Thief*, the newspapers will say.) She is seated against a front window of the terminal, taxis and private cars moving sluggishly beyond her in the gathering darkness; she seems engrossed in a book. A seat beside her is empty, and the man occupies it.

"I've been looking for you," he says.

She glances at him with no sort of recognition. "I don't know you," she says.

"Sure you do."

She sighs and puts the book aside. "Is this all you characters think about?—picking up girls like we were stray animals? What do you think I am?"

"You lifted my wallet," he says. He is pleased to have said "lifted," thinking it sounds more worldly than *stole* or *took* or even *ripped off*.

"I beg your pardon?" the girl says.

"I know you did—at the magazine counter. If you'll just give it back, we can forget the whole thing. If you don't, then I'll hand you over to the police."

She studies him, her face serious. "All right," she says. She pulls the black bag onto her lap, reaches into it and draws out a wallet.

He takes it from her. "Wait a minute," he says. "This isn't mine."

The girl runs; he bolts after her. It is like a scene in a movie—bystanders scattering, the girl zig-zagging to avoid collisions, the sound of his own breathing reminding him how old he is—until he hears a woman's voice behind him:

"Stop, thief! Stop that man!"

Ahead of him the brunette disappears around a corner and in the same moment a young man in a marine uniform puts out a foot to trip him up. He falls hard, banging knee and elbow on the tile floor of the terminal, but manages to hang on to the wallet which is not his.

The wallet is a woman's, fat with money and credit cards from places like Sak's and I. Magnin and Lord & Taylor, and it belongs to the blonde in the fur-trimmed coat—the blonde he has earlier seen in conversation with the criminal brunette. She, too, is breathless, as is the policeman with her.

"That's him," the blonde girl says. "He lifted my billfold."

It occurs to the man that he cannot even prove his own identity to the policeman.

Two weeks later—the embarrassment and rage have diminished, the family lawyer has been paid, the confusion in his household has receded—the wallet turns up without explanation in one morning's mail. It is intact, no money is missing, all the cards are in place. Though he is relieved, the man thinks that for the rest of his life he will feel guilty around policemen, and ashamed in the presence of women.

Artists and Their Models

KATHLEEN hated to be photographed, and so of course they had been living at the farm scarcely two months when she looked up one morning from her breakfast—a bowl of shredded wheat—to discover Alan standing in the kitchen doorway with the old Ikoflex, its twin lenses staring at her like the eyes of an owl with its head cocked to one side.

"Alan, no," she said, and she raised one hand, the hand holding the spoon, to shield herself from the camera.

"Just keep on doing what you were doing," he said.

"No," she said. "I don't want you taking my picture; you know I don't like it."

She could not explain it, though she had tried more than once to find reasons acceptable to those friends whose hobby consisted of stalking fellow humans and capturing their images on film. "I'm not worth it," she would say. "Don't waste your film on me. You'll break your poor camera." Grudgingly her friends would unframe her and turn to other subjects; as time passed, she had come to believe powerfully that she was not photogenic. It was almost like a fear—like the superstition of primitives who do not wish their souls stolen.

"I mean it," she said to Alan. "Put that camera away or I'll walk out."

Perhaps it was that her father had made too much of her when she was a sweet-faced child with long, honey-blonde hair and innocent green eyes. In the albums at her mother's house

31

were hundreds of photographs he had taken of her—baptism, birthday parties, scenes at the mountains and lakes, the biennial family reunions—all of them seeming now unfamiliar, like pictures of a younger sister whose clothes were handed down, whose hairdos were slightly out of fashion. She remembered that her father had photographed her even on the morning of his death, when she was eleven; they had just come home from a picnic—the month was July—and on the last pages of the last album were pictures of her taking the wicker picnic basket from the tailgate of the station wagon, of her mother posed in front of the porch holding her hand, of a slightly askew father (her mother had snapped the picture) standing behind her with his arms around her waist. This last remembered photo haunted her: her father was smiling, but it was—she saw now—not so much his own expression as death's, the teeth sharply defined, the mouth thin, the eyes far back in their sockets as if gauging the world through the wrong end of binoculars. It was a frightening image. That afternoon he had stood just inside her room and stared at her for a long moment as if he intended to tell her something; then he fell against the dresser and slid to the floor, his heart stopped. *No more cameras*, she thought. *That's enough of that.* Though in truth she wasn't sure her dislike of being photographed had anything to do with her father. Anyway, now it was fourteen years later, and it was her lover standing in the doorway.

"Please, Alan."

Finally he put the camera aside. He sat across from her at the oak table and studied her. "It's snowing," he said.

"Then go take pictures of the snow." She ate the last thin spoonful of sweetened milk from the bowl, and laid the spoon down. "Isn't this supposed to be writing time for you?"

"Oh, sure," he said. "I was feeling restless, a little blocked. I thought we ought to have some sort of pictorial record of the time we spend here—snapshots of the house, the charming occupants, the dogs and cats."

"Take everything else," she said. "Don't waste your film on me; you'll break your poor camera."

He sat quietly, his chin rested on his right hand, his left hand fiddling with the metal lens cap on the Ikoflex. She cleared away the cereal dish and spoon, ran water over them in the pantry sink.

"Do you want some coffee?" she said.

"No. Too early for me."

"I can't survive without coffee in the morning." She said that to him at least once every day—as pattern, as ritual? Here she was, apparently structuring the relations between them, and yet she was suspicious of cameras. She sat at the table with her coffee. Alan was still studying her.

"You're an awfully pretty woman," he said. "You ought to be pleased to have yourself on film."

"No," she said. She sipped the coffee—a bit stronger than she liked it; she could not, even after two months, be sure about the house percolator, how much coffee to feed it, how long to leave it heating. She thought that if Alan were not twice her age he would not flatter her, would realize that what he imagined to be prettiness was merely youth. She put out her hand to him and caressed one side of his face, his scraggly new beard. "You're sweet to think so," she said.

He rubbed his cheek against her hand and closed his eyes. "What are you up to this morning?"

"Well," she said, trying to make her voice stern, "assuming you're really going to go upstairs and work, and not prance around the house bothering people with your little black box, I think I'll take a shower and dry my hair—and probably water the plants. Then we'll have lunch and decide what's next." She took her hand away from him. "I don't approve of this casual carrying on," she said.

"Cruel child," he said.

When he had gone back upstairs, so she could once more hear the typewriter and be certain he would not ambush her with the camera, she freshened her coffee and sat for a while at the table, feeling lazy—or, better, languid—letting her vision be filled with the slow light from the farmyard. It was a solemn, steady sort of storm, large-flaked and nearly windless; the pickup truck they used was already transformed into some tall-cabbed carriage that awaited the harnessing of a team. The snowflakes were as stark as she could imagine; the spaces between them and among them seemed blue, like twilight or a shadowed cloud. What was Alan's passion for freezing the world in his words and, now, his pictures? Kathleen saw the world as fluid, moving, something that carried her with it toward an unknowable morrow; he seemed to see it as made of discrete pieces, capturable, to be dissected and analyzed and rearranged to suit himself. Did life really not elude him? At times she chided him for living in the past—and yet she realized that because she was twenty-five it was natural for him to remember being that same age in a time *when she was not even born*. Perhaps that was why he wanted her picture—to suspend her in her youth against a future when she, too, would be fifty. But that would be terrible; she wanted never to see herself from that distance. If it was bad to be old—and sometimes Alan talked grimly of his own mortality—how much worse it would be to keep all the reminders of having been young.

As if being young were so marvelous anyway. Upstairs, slipping out of Alan's robe—she rolled the sleeves almost halfway up, and Alan never unrolled them, looking always as though he had outgrown the garment—she caught the image of her youthful self in the blistered oval mirror of the bathroom. The image had never entirely pleased her; she thought her breasts too small, her hips too heavy, her legs too short. Nothing quite touched the proper design she wished for her body.

What often perplexed her about her connection with Alan was his evident blindness to her flaws. Standing under the makeshift shower whose water pressure was less than she wanted but as much as the pump in the cellar could rise to, Kathleen marveled at the man's capacity for praise, how he seemed never to have enough of telling her how pretty she was, how each time they made love the discovery of her flesh seemed to him as remarkable as the first time he had undressed her. Surely he was not pretending; surely, after nearly a year together, she would know if he was pretending. No other man in her life had ever made so much of her.

She shampooed her hair, breathing the scent of apricot, feeling with her fingers how much longer her hair was, how much more difficult to deal with it was becoming—because Alan liked it long, and she wanted to please him. She thought of a friend at college—what was her name? the tall girl with the reddish hair who went off to San Francisco—the girl who lived with a much older man even though he told her he wanted her to gain forty pounds because he liked plump women. *That* would be more than she could do for anyone, even Alan. The girl had gained twenty; met the man half way. Love—or sex, or whatever it was—was bizarre. Or only bizarre between generations. Did Alan see her as Kathleen? Or only as Young Woman who differed from women of his own age?

Drying herself, toweling her hair, she stood as close as she could to the black stovepipe that passed through the bathroom on its way from the woodstove in the kitchen to the brick chimney. The room was not uncomfortable in winter—though she had feared it would be when she arrived in October and first saw the inside of the farmhouse. And a small space heater stood nearby if she wanted to use it; today she had not, for she was about to be extravagant with the hair dryer and Alan had warned her about the bills from the Hydro. Now she stood under its whine, brushing and pausing, coaxing the hair which fell now nearly to her shoulders to tip under instead of—naturally—curling outward at the ends. The old mirror gave back her imperfect figure, the breasts thin, the thighs bulky—"My God," he said to her again and again, "my dear God, how stunning you

are," stroking her belly, the inside of her thighs, "how absolutely stunning"—even her mouth a little large for her own notions of fitness.

Once Alan had said to her—they were walking hand in hand
along the narrow graveled road that led from the farm to the
main highway: "Men, you know, always think of themselves as
ugly when they're naked. It's as if everything would be fine if
they could just keep the fig leaf on, but strip that away and they
feel uneasy—a bit grotesque, I'd call it."

"Women think that way, too," she had said.

"Yes, I've read that, and I don't understand it." He'd
pressed her hand hard. "Don't you ever dare feel like that."

"Sometimes I do," she had said.

He stopped and hugged her tightly against him. "No, no," he
said. "No, no, no."

So it was absurd to doubt him. Wasn't it? She switched off
the hair dryer and set it beside the sink; now the house seemed
strangely silent. She listened. She could not hear the sound of
Alan's typewriter, and she imagined him perched before the
machine, scowling and pulling abstractedly at his beard, hung
up on some abstruse philosophical muddle that had just come
unexpectedly out of the mouth of one of his characters. He went
into the study each morning at seven, sharp—as if to fail at his
routines might imply a larger failure—and stayed at least until
eleven, sometimes longer, but often long silences broke in on the
clatter of his work. Then, likely as not, he would come out for
coffee, or to complain to her about some disturbance she was
guilty of, or to get "a fresh perspective" by doing something
irrelevant—like annoying her with the Ikoflex and the threat of
fixing her imperfections on film.

She looked out the window, pulling the robe around her and
knotting the belt. No, there he was, down in the farmyard with
the two dogs, throwing snowballs at them and encouraging
them to romp into the great snowbank building slowly on the lee
side of the pickup. She smiled; he was like a schoolboy, happy
because a blizzard has shut down classes.

"When I'm dead"—she heard him saying this like an echo from one day when he had seemed unusually gloomy—"When I'm dead, you'll still be a young woman."

Kathleen put the words out of her mind and went down the narrow hallway toward the bedroom. The door to the study was ajar; it was on the south side of the house, lighter than the bathroom or kitchen—as if it were overlooking fair weather while the storm raged at the other windows.

She pushed the door further open and looked in. It was a bad habit of hers, she knew, to be curious about what Alan was doing, what he was writing, and she found herself entering the room and going to the typewriter on its gray stand under the window. A sheet of yellow paper was in the machine, but it was blank—not even a page number. She was about to pick up one of a sheaf of papers beside the typewriter when her attention was caught by several larger sheets nestled on a shelf of the bookcase nearby. She slid them out and saw at once that they were sketches—done in ink and pencil—of her.

She knelt in front of the bookcase and spread the sheets, fan-like, before her. There were a half-dozen in all, some pages with two or three drawings on them, some with large sketches that took up most of the sheet. Yes, they were all *her;* she had not imagined Alan could draw—and certainly would not have imagined his choosing her as a subject. Had she ever seen him sketching? No, not at all. Then these were from his mind's eye, from his remembering. Here she was drying her hair, her head tilted, the dryer held high in a hand that bent gracefully at the wrist, the brush in her other hand lifting a fall of hair at the nape of her neck, the sleeves of the robe rolled up—yes, exactly so. Here she was at the kitchen table, reading, her forehead serene but her lips pursed, her right elbow on the table beside the book and the hand in mid-air, floating. And—

And here she was naked! with the brass skeleton of the big bed in the corner room behind her, her hair tousled from sleep and her breasts bared above the bed linen, their gauntness, their overlarge aureoles. She turned the drawing paper face down, but the next sheet was worse still—several small sketches in pencil of herself in bed, in postures of loving. They were not obscene—she was willing to concede that—but surely indiscreet, much too detailed: the look on her face, the knuckle of her left hand pressed against her mouth, the right hand clenched in the hair of her belly—

She shut her eyes. *All right*, she said to herself; *all right*. She opened her eyes and turned the sheets face up, arranged so that she could look at all of them—two rows, three pages in each.

No—she studied them—no, they weren't so bad. She had never looked at herself this way. Her dissatisfactions with her body were founded not so much on what she thought of herself, but on what she thought of other women; she felt, simply, that she fell short of this or that standard of beauty—to the point of jealousy, to the point of being made miserable by the sight of a pretty model in a women's magazine. But here, in these drawings, without comparing herself— Yes, she rather liked herself. The line of her breasts had a delicacy that belonged somehow to the way she thought of her personality; her thighs were not so much heavy as they were womanly—she was not some hollow-eyed, strung-out New York mannequin popping diet pills to keep a career. And the way she carried herself on these pages: the tilt of her head, the angles and planes of her shoulders and arms and hands— She sat back on her heels. The discovery of Alan's drawings was a revelation to her, and at the same time a confusion. While she was oddly grateful to him for seeing her as she had never before thought to see herself, yet she felt betrayed, spied on, somehow *used*.

When she had dressed and come down to the kitchen, Alan was standing at the window by the woodstove, both hands around a mug of coffee, gazing out at the falling snow. He was wearing the white cable-stitch sweater his wife had knitted him; his mackinaw was draped over the back of one of the kitchen chairs, snow melting from it onto the linoleum. She took her own cup from the table and went to freshen it.

"Wind's starting to come up," Alan said. "The dogs go wild in this weather."

She sat at the table and sipped the warmed coffee.

"What's the matter?" he said.

"I didn't know you could draw."

"Oh." He sat across the table from her. "Sounds like you were in the study."

"I looked in," she said. "I wondered why I wasn't hearing the noise of honest labor." She realized she was about to act bitchy, and she watched him gathering his resources against her. He would have to defend himself if she pressed her charge that he was being lazy, if she argued that he had abused her fondness. At the same time, she knew it would be difficult for him not to chastise her for snooping among his papers.

"Are you offended?" he said.

She shook her head. "I was at first—when I first found the drawings—but I think you intended to flatter me." Alan said nothing. She looked at him. "Did you?"

"I didn't intend anything. I was only trying to be truthful about you."

"I see." She thought she did see—but if that were so, why was she waiting for him to say more? It was as if she were setting a trap for him.

"I'm pleased you were flattered," he said, "but that doesn't explain the way you're behaving."

"How am I behaving?"

"Cold," he said.

"I don't know what it is," Kathleen said. "I guess I feel as if my space has been invaded. Not maliciously—I don't think you'd do anything to me with malice—but as if the notion of privacy had never crossed your mind."

"That isn't so," Alan said. "I'm sensitive to privacy. I certainly respect *yours*."

"I didn't mean that you don't let me have the bathroom to myself," she said.

Alan studied her. She could see the muscles working at the corners of his jaw—he clenched his teeth, a nervous habit having to do with stress or frustration, and ordinarily she would have reached across to him, touched one side of his face, and said gently: "No, don't grit your teeth."—and she wondered what was going through his mind, if he so badly wanted to say: *What about my own privacy?*

"You remind me of my father," she said.

"I had the idea you were fond of your father," he said.

She thought what a true thing she had just said—how both men took advantage of her loving them, pouting, sulking, turning her own words and feelings back on herself as if they refused to be loved except according to their own rules; how she would have died if her father hadn't loved her, but that when he came into her room without knocking, or when he said *Look here, kitten* and took her picture with the green leatherette camera he once bought her for her birthday, she almost hated him; how when she was treated by either man as if she were a prized possession she felt both insulted and guilty, knowing she ought somehow to love back, no matter what.

"That isn't the point," she said.

"Then what is?"

She felt helpless, as if she were wilting, as if none of the new things she had learned about herself were translatable into language a man understood. "I don't know."

"Anyway," Alan said, "you have to remember I was up here five weeks by myself, with nothing of you except phone calls— except your voice from a thousand miles off. I did the drawings as a kind of homage. I wanted you. I wanted to remind myself of how special you are."

"That pleases me, Alan. Truly."

"Then stop giving me hell." He went silent, fumbling self-consciously at the beard he was not yet accustomed to. Kathleen noticed it was always his chin he touched, where the beard had come in shockingly gray. She wanted to be honest and unkind, to say to him: *You can't hide it.*

"Well it's all very lovely," she said. "I expect I'll see this whole year written down someplace—with illustrations—and you'll be the hero." She stood up from the table. "I think I should get lunch, and you should work."

He came into the pantry behind her and put his arms around her waist. "Dear Kitten," he murmured into her hair, "you know you have to make allowances for my advancing years."

"I try," she said, but she wondered—if he were so wise, so concerned to stop the world for his inspection—why he didn't understand that he was asking for sympathy, not love. Then, later in the day when she was standing at the back door to put down food for the dogs and cats, she realized how important it was that Alan had not put himself into any of the pictures she had found.

Pieces of String

---

1. Crossings

BEFORE I was born—I think I had not even been conceived—my mother and my father were on a motor trip through Québec province in a 1928 Studebaker Dictator. They were on their way to Ste. Anne de Beaupré, but their journey was interrupted by an accident. It was at night, the road was narrow and rutted, my father had not driven this way before. Ascending the crest of a small hill and careering down its further slope at a speed of close to twenty-five miles an hour, he collided heavily with a cow—one of a sizeable herd being driven across the highway from pasture.

I have heard this story told by my parents uncountable times throughout my growing up. What is strongest in my father's mind is the image of the cow lying on her back with her four legs stiffly raised, and the Studebaker's headlights sending their dusty beams likewise straight up because the cow had kicked them. What my mother remembers most vividly is the lantern of the herdsman, several hundred feet away in the meadow, dancing and shivering with the anger of the man as he ran shouting toward the road.

This shows the difference between my father and my mother.

2. *A Story with Sex and Violence*

I WAS standing at the bedroom window, making a telephone
call to a friend in the East. While I was placing the call—
giving numbers to the operator, waiting out the clicks and
buzzes—I saw that my neighbor's dog was chasing a chicken in
the field that separates our two houses. My neighbor's wife has
been raising chickens for about six months now, and she has—or
has had—as many as twenty or thirty of the things. They're
very large. It's always impressed me, how large they all are.
Very large and very white. Anyway, the dog, which is a hunting
dog—some sort of mottled spaniel—was pursuing this chicken.
At first it was comic. Chickens are not graceful; they run
awkwardly, and when they change direction they make a clumsy
movement with their wings—an exaggerated shrug of the shoulders—and look as if they're about to fall apart into a confusion of
feathers and skinny feet. So here was my neighbor's dog chasing
my neighbor's wife's chicken, back and forth, back and forth,
and me waiting for the connection to be made to the phone of my
friend, and it's a warm day, a very windy day in late October—
most unseasonable, a most benign bit of weather—so that the
whole world outside the bedroom window appears to be in motion—the tall dead grasses shivering and the cottonwood tree
swaying and dry leaves being driven down to earth. And the dog
and the chicken. And then all at once the dog *catches* the
chicken. It startled me, his catching it. Caught it in his jaws
right behind its silly head, then hoisted it off the ground and
began running away with it. Out of the field, up and down my
neighbor's driveway, prancing with that gawky huge chicken,
shaking it. My God. And then he drops it, leaves the chicken
lying in the gravel of the driveway, motionless. I thought: *Good
God, he's killed it.* And he had. Killed it dead. Just then my
friend came on the line. *Hello,* I said, *I've just watched my*

neighbor's dog chase a big white chicken and kill it. She said:
That's very interesting. I just ate chicken for dinner. Do you
suppose it's the same one? I said I thought everything was
possible, and I was trying to think of something funny to say
when I noticed the dog was after another chicken. I said: *My*
God, he's chasing another one. She said: *Can't you stop him?*
And I said: *I don't want to get involved.* We both laughed like
fools.

3. *Fashion*

E RIC WORTH had never owned a suit that really *fit* him, so
one day, when he was stationed with the army in Wies-
baden, he went to a German tailor and had his measurements
taken. He picked out a fabric from among several bolts of English wool, then for weeks he lay awake after all the barracks
lights were out and imagined how he would look when the suit
was finished. He would look exceptional.

He pictured himself wearing the suit, feeling it move with
him, knowing it would wear all his life because it was *his*—not
an article made for some approximation of himself whose name
was irrelevant and whose round shoulders were matters of indif-
ference to the cutting machine. He saw himself on furlough,
looking impeccable and British, strolling into the Hotel
Vierjahreszeiten in Hamburg—a hotel where they did not wel-
come Americans because it was the Americans who had done
the old bombing—smoking perhaps an oval cigarette or, even
better, one of those Russian *papyrosi* that smelled like a trash
fire, holding the cigarette like Franchot Tone in the early morning movies, between the thumb and the first two fingers with
the palm up, the other hand slipped casually and lightly into the
pocket of his suitjacket. He saw himself in the hotel dining

room, at a small table near a window—one Martini, the lobster with a Riesling he would let the steward choose, cognac and a leisurely smoke afterward. Not far away, a handsome, blonde, thirtyish woman admiring the well-dressed foreigner. . . .

When the suit was finished and the tailor sent a message to the barracks: "Herr Worth, your suit is ready," he couldn't pay for it, couldn't scrape together the eighty dollars he had committed himself to. He was too embarrassed to face the tailor—the man lived in a tiny apartment above a jeweler's shop—to climb the narrow staircase and say to the German that he had broken his promise, that he could not pay. In the end he sent his buddy David Darby to the tailor. Darby was about the same size; the tailor altered the suit—*his* suit—and it fit David Darby as if he were a man with no name at all, as if the suit were machine-cut but altered as best could be to the shape of David Darby's approximate self. But Eric could never bring himself to imagine David Darby leaving the Vierjahreszeiten with the handsome blonde woman on his arm.

As it turned out, the only clothes he bought in Europe were not new at all; they belonged to Corporal Nordstrom. When Nordstrom was killed in a motorcycle accident on the Autobahn, his clothes were auctioned off in the dayroom. Eric bought a gray suit for nine dollars, had it altered by the base tailor, and wore it frequently for many years. His wife never referred to it except as "Eric's dead man's suit."

4. Children

WHEN she was twenty-two years old they said to her: "You can't have children." She believed them—the family doctor and the specialist he consulted with—and came to terms with what she thought of then as a fortunate incapacity. Three years later, in Philadelphia, she broke off her engagement to a selfish young man at the welfare agency where she worked, and the pattern of her life was established as rigidly as if it had been set in a matrix of stone.

Much, much later, after her fortieth birthday and when she had for the first time in her life decided to take a real lover, she was suddenly perplexed by what the doctors had said. Now she wondered what they had meant by "can't." Had they meant she was barren—for so, she came to think, she had led her life— or had they actually meant to say only that the process of child-bearing would be too difficult for her with her slightness, her small pelvis, the binding muscles of her thighs whose tense strength puzzled her? How, after all, had they said those words? "You *can't* have children," with the deep stress on the auxiliary to action? or "You can't *have* children," stressing the act, the bearing itself? She could not remember. Perhaps they had put the stress on herself, implying that she had been singled out from thousands of small and pretty young women as one especially disfavored. Or perhaps the important word was "children"; it was all right for her to have anything—horses, parakeets, husbands, careers—*except*.

The family doctor was long dead; she could not recall the name of the specialist. She found her present ignorance absurd, and the absurdity of it colored the affair—probably her last, with a man fifteen years younger than she—from its very begin-ning. In the car—her car—driving to a motel in this new city before the two of them had ever slept together, the question presented itself.

"Listen," he had said, as if she might not, "could you stop at a drugstore somewhere?"

"What for?" She was working her way through traffic, north-bound on the Outer Drive, muddling nervously from lane to lane and trying to concentrate on her driving.

"Well—shouldn't I take some precaution, or something?"

"Don't worry," she said. But almost as soon as the words were out, she was sorry for the tone of them—brusque, so impatient they must have seemed crotchety. She recognized that the man—the *young* man—was embarrassed to have had to speak at all of such a thing.

"Of course I'll worry," he said. He cast an odd look at her. "You don't want a baby, do you?"

"Oh, *please*," she said, and she had accelerated recklessly across three busy lanes of the Drive because she was drawing close to the exit nearest the motel and she was frightened that her anger would keep her from seeing it in time.

5. *Mothers*

ONE Monday morning after her son has gone to school she finds a prophylactic in the top right-hand drawer of his dresser. She shows it to his father, her husband.

"Look," she says. "Look at this."

"I see," he says. He has put aside the morning paper and set down the spoon he used to stir sugar into his coffee.

"What should we do about it?"

"What do you *want* to do?"

She looks at the small square she holds in her fingers. It is glossy and gold. "I thought you should talk to him."

"I wouldn't know what to say. *My* mother found one of those when I was thirteen—a lot younger than he is."

"Is that true?"

"It's something boys did. You had a friend who worked in a drugstore, and he was the one who could steal safes for you. We called them *safes*, short for safeties." He thinks back. Nowadays the prophylactics are out in the open, visible and various—colored, ribbed, spined. "Maybe it just makes him feel worldly."

"But maybe he's using them," she says.

Her husband sips his coffee. "Then thank your stars," he says.

6. *The Hundred Steps*

A Found Story

MY sister and I had a friend who was in her eighth month. Her parents were going up to Bethel for the weekend; she wanted to go with them, so she asked her doctor if it would be all right for her to ride as far as that and he thought yes, it would be fine. What did they do the next morning but get into their car and start for the White Mountains. They stopped at a place where you had to climb a hundred stairs and back up the same number to see the wonders. The daughter was determined to go down with them. They had to start very early the next morning for Brunswick and just did get home when the baby was born, but it was dead. Her mother told us it was pretty and had quite a lot of hair.

Wasps

S HE noticed the wasp nest on a Saturday afternoon in late July when she was mowing the lawn. It was at the east end of the house, high up under the overhang where the two roof surfaces met at the ridgepole, and it didn't amount to much yet—just a gray-celled beginning to the nest, perhaps no more than three or four inches across. The wasps were busy at it, like fervent homemakers, all their dangerous, poisonous temperament set aside for domestic preoccupations. She could see a half-dozen of the hard-jacketed insects hovering far above her, idling in and out of the shadow from a sun just starting its downward slide to the northwest.

She paused in her work to study the nest, the power mower running loudly and clouding the air with unpleasant blue smoke. The mower needed attention—it was pale green, and heaven only knew how many other colors the mower company had used on newer and newer models—it had not been adjusted in four years; if she could not persuade the man she lived with to tend to this earthbound machinery, how might she coax him to rid her of the wasp nest?

He stood beside her, looking up, shielding his eyes as if from brightness even though the sun was halfway down to the horizon on the other side of the house.

"They've been busy," he said.

"Can you get it down?"

He shook his head. He looked down at the ground, at the cut grass dying under his feet—under his slippers. "I don't think we can hit it with the hose. It's way up there, and the water pressure's not very strong."

"You might reach it with the ladder," she said.

"I don't know. I'm not sure I want to get that close to them. I've heard of people that died from wasp stings—wasp venom or something."

"I have, too," she said. She studied the man. Sometimes she thought if she could look *hard* enough, if she could only see past whatever that pale covering was that seemed to be a youthful, regular-featured face, she might find the right button to push, switch to turn, to move him to—anything.

"You know what I think we should do," the man said.

"What?"

"I think we should just wait until winter, when it's so cold they can't function. Then we can knock the nest down and burn it."

"We could do that."

"That's what we did at the other house."

That's what *I* did, she thought. And it was far easier there; the nest was scarcely ten feet off the ground, fastened to the eaves above their bedroom window. They hadn't noticed it until December, and she knocked it down the same day, to be sure the wasps wouldn't come back.

"The lawn looks nice," the man said. He went around the back of the house, headed toward the screened porch. She could hear baseball voices from the television set he had moved from the living room to the porch.

Monday morning on her way to work she discovered a wasp inside the car and she had to stop at the side of the road, terrified of being stung, until she was able to force it out the window. It had long, trailing legs like thin landing gear that brushed the back of her hand as it flew into the sunlight and rose swiftly straight up and out of her sight.

At work she spread the telephone book open on her desk and turned the classified pages until she came to *Exterminating and Fumigating*. There were several names, only one of them not the franchise of some national company. She decided she would call that one; on her coffee break she went to the public phone in the lobby of her building and dialed the number. A woman answered.

"I'm sorry," the voice told her, "but he won't be home until evening. Usually he comes home to have lunch, but today's especially busy. He's checking out that new apartment project on the other side of town."

"May I leave my number?"

"Certainly, dear." The woman at the other end of the line sighed as if being careful to write the number precisely. "I'll have him call you."

She was picking up the supper dishes when the telephone rang. The man answered it; he was in the kitchen, making himself an after-supper highball.

"It's for you," he said.

She set the dishes at the side of the kitchen sink and took the phone from him. "Yes," she said into it.

"This is the exterminator," said a man's voice. It was deep and clear, a voice the woman liked. "You left your number."

"I did," she said. "Thank you for calling."

"What's the trouble?"

"Wasps," she told him. "A nest of them under the eaves." She hesitated; the exterminator, from his end, said nothing for several seconds, and she wondered if he expected her to draw out the whole explanation of why she could not get at the wasp nest, why the man she lived with could not help, how afraid she was of insects, of heights—everything.

He finally spoke. "Go on," he said.

"I think it would be easier if you could just come out to the house and look for yourself." She started to give him the address, but he interrupted her.

"It would save you money if you could explain it to me. If I have to drive out, I have to charge you for an extra call—an estimate."

"No," she said. "It isn't a question of money."

"Who was that on the phone?" the man she lived with said later, when she freshened his drink for him.

"The exterminator, about the wasp nest."

"He sounded like a foreigner." The man took a sip from his drink and settled back, watching a boxing match on television. As an apparent afterthought he said: "I thought we were going to wait for cold weather."

"I decided not to," she said.

She started the dishwasher. The machine vibrated and screamed and spotted her dishes; every two or three weeks it blew its fuse, but it was all she had. She had proposed to the man that they simply stop using the machine—that instead they take turns doing the dishes by hand—but he had seemed unattracted to the idea. She wondered whatever she could do as she made a comfortable corner for herself at the end of the sofa, drawing her legs up and opening the novel she had begun weeks ago.

"Perhaps he *does* sound foreign," she said idly.

The exterminator drove out to the house on the following Saturday morning. He was a tall man, heavy-set but not fat, and she imagined as she watched him walk toward her from the dark blue panel truck that he might be—what? Oriental? Polynesian? But she did not think of them as *big*, or as *impressive*. He came into the opened garage and knocked at the kitchen door. She had just finished emptying the dishwasher and was beginning to refill the machine with the morning's breakfast dishes. The man was in the living room, drinking coffee and watching cartoons.

"Someone's at the garage door," the man called.

"I know." She opened the door. The exterminator bent his head toward her—was he actually bowing?—and held out a small white card.

"I came about the wasps," he said.

She took the card; it carried his name and telephone number. "Come in," she said. She led him into the bright kitchen. "I'm in the middle of getting rid of the breakfast mess. Will you have a cup of coffee?"

He looked about him. He had dark, large eyes, and they seemed to take in everything, like camera lenses, as if the room were somehow memorable. He noticed the pitcher on the counter beside the refrigerator.

"Is that orange juice?"

"Yes."

He smiled; his teeth were astonishingly white. "I'd rather have a little of that."

She poured a glass and handed it to him. He held the glass against the light from the kitchen windows. "You ought to check your water softener," he said. He sat at the table and drained the glass, setting it down with clear satisfaction.

"Better than coffee," he said. "Coffee raises cain with the nervous system."

She took the glass from the exterminator just as the man she lived with came out to the kitchen. He was still wearing his striped pajamas.

"More coffee," he told her. "Good morning," he said to the exterminator. "You must be the man about the wasp crisis."

"That's so."

"I was going to take care of them when I got the chance, but she—" He gestured toward the woman. "She's so bloody impatient."

She filled the cup and gave it back to him. For a moment he

stood with it as if he had something further to say, then he turned and went to the living room.

"Shall we go look?" the woman said.

The two of them stood at the end of the house, looking up. The wasps wheeled and darted about the nest, its size slowly increasing, the cells deeper and clearer than they had been a week earlier when she first noticed it. She thought the exterminator was not going to speak, and she wondered if he felt he had wasted his time, if her problem were too trivial to engage his interest.

"Is he your husband?"

The question surprised her without offending her.

"No," she said. "He's the man I'm living with." In ordinary circumstances she would simply have said Yes—all the neighbors believed them married—but lying seemed inappropriate. In any case she had lived with the man for so long, four years, that the name of the relationship seemed beside the point.

"He's young." The exterminator moved away from her, his attention still given to the wasp nest above them.

"He is," she agreed. What more could she say to a man who really had no business commenting on her life? And what difference did it make—to anyone—if after her divorce she had one day found herself drawn to a man ten years her junior? Besides, she was barely thirty-five; she was herself still young.

"I could probably come out next week," the exterminator said. "Tuesday or Wednesday. I'll phone before I drive out."

"I'd be grateful," she said. "Do you need me to be here?"

"Just so someone's here. I don't like no one to be at home. People are funny; they think we do things to their houses."

"One of us will be here," she said. "I work until 3:30 or so."

They were walking now, away from the end of the house where the wasps were building, into the back yard where the two new maples stood. The trees were transplanted from the

A Fear of Children

W E meet in the hallway of the liberal arts building, at the end of a wainscoted corridor with the greenish sunlight making our faces mossy. She is hugging music books; they barricade her figure up to her neck.

"I dreamed about you last night," she says.

"No kidding?" I say. Her black hair seems caught back by the fragile wings of her ears, but somewhere at the nape of her neck is a ribbon-bow.

"I stole your umbrella," she says. "We were inside a railroad station with a lot of tall glass, and everybody was watching me."

"But you pinched the umbrella just the same." I finish her line of thought, her breathy discourse. I have a class to get to.

"*Your* umbrella."

"And what for?"

"I don't know. I woke up." She hitches the music books up against her blouse-front. "I know what it means," she says, and she moves past me out of the swimming pool sunlight, her thin body brushing my arm and carrying a slight borrowing of my pulse away with her. The white hair-ribbon is two grace notes.

She is a crazy girl.

When I make love to her on the spruced slopes that fall away from the old chapel, I am terrified. At such times she is a woman who seems manufactured wholly of sounds, as if there were in the world a factory devoted to musical instruments, and she is a computer accident which has run all the assembly lines harmoniously together at the far side of craftsmanship. She is all reeds and strings and percussive surface. I never know if I am pleasing her or hurting her, and I say, after the night and the humid wind have fallen to silence: "Darling, are you all right?" and she always whispers: "Yes, I liked it, yes."

She is a singer, an artist. She has so lovely a soprano voice that I am sure she will destroy it; this scholars' world has no place for it, no competency to train it or do anything but catch hold of it and ride it into the particular oblivion she will eventually aim it toward. I am being tragic—as I always am when I think of her.

We talk about differences between thought and deed. I ask when she is under me on the melting lawns what she is thinking; I ask, to hear her answer with her mad wordless music, and at the end of that we talk.

"I think about dying," she says, "and floating in space, listening to all the voices." I remember her belief—that all the sounds humanity has made since time began reverberate in the eternity she imagines. "I make myself outsing them."

"I think about machines," I say.

"You engineers," she scolds. "All your wheels are loose." She rolls away from me, and all I can reach are the tips of her fingers in the grass.

Not me is insane. She.

When she learns her madness, some indescribable spring morning when I am not with her, she will make a song of it. Song is her reason for everything, the reason ample enough to contain unreason. Whatever she does, she does because she cannot sing every moment of her life. She tells me over and over, angrily, about the limitations of voice, and I remind her of my machineries and the science of the voice-box. She scowls at me. Voice—song and the manipulations of song—is the matrix of nerve and muscle shaping all her actions.

We have one class in common this summer, on the top floor of

Urschel Hall. We rise to the classroom by an elevator, where we kiss if we ride alone, and hold hands if we share the space with strangers. Of all unlikely subjects, it is the Russian language we study together. Does she believe she will sing Tatyana or Lizavyeta, I cannot tell; I am in the course for curiosity and technology. Every morning from ten to eleven we sit in the penthouse of Urschel while Katerina Evgenevna drills us, rehearses us, implicates us in the tangles of the Russian verb. I sit behind my love at the back of the room, and as Katerina Evgenevna overbears us by turns I am leaned forward to blow gently the wisps of hair which have escaped her ribbon, to whisper improprieties I know her eyes close to look at, to stroke with the very tips of my fingers the gooseflesh of her upper arm. No one sees my attentions; we live in an ignorant world. After class, as we are waiting for the elevator, I squeeze her hand and say a tender "Golubochka" into her hair. She shakes her ponytail and scowls away from me. "God, what an ugly language," she says.

We talk at lunch. So persistent are her dreams that when I ask real questions I am never sure of real answers. She wishes she had loved her mother; her mother was a miraculous coloratura; she feeds upon guilt for her mother's failure and suicide. I see, in my mind's myopic eye, her angelic mother mute in the bubble of eternity, adding her silent arias to the universe of the dead. I imagine it is her mother she looks for whenever she tips back her head, her eyes shut, answering my questions.

On the last evening of the summer session there is a concert—a brief ballet, a string quartet, a few recital voices. She is one of the singers, and so we are separated for the evening. I see her for a moment outside the auditorium where summer students and their parents mill about us. The air is heavy and warm. She wears a sleeveless dress, white with enormous splashes of orange flowers that explode like suns among the dull ticket buyers.

"You knock their eyes out," I tell her.

"I'm after their ears," she says.

I sit in the third row, center, sweating and embarrassed to be alone, reading the mimeographed program over and over; her name is misspelled. In the dark hall I am tolerant of the quartet, amused by the lady cellist. The ballet is dissonant and stimulating; it contains an idyllic *pas de deux* sweetly erotic— tactile and copulative and delicate as snakes. I close my senses to the first three singers, waiting for my love.

She is stunning. In the vivid spotlight she seems dead, pale and sharp-boned, and she keeps her hands folded before her flowers. I am astonished that she sings in Russian—out of one corner of my eye I catch sight of Katerina Evgenevna nodding and smiling because the accent is so right. She sings "The Snow- storm" as it was never meant to be sung—delicate, slow. The lover calls to his lady as in a solemn dance, the snowflakes drift- ing languidly, the man and the woman running like figures in one of her ascendant dreams. Then she sings "Birches." The dreary audience weeps, and applauds for three minutes.

All that night we lie together. The dormitory is nearly de- serted; to arrange her presence in my room for the first time is not difficult, and we hug each other hard to keep from rolling out of the narrow bed. The windows are open. Below us on the flagstones a farewell party is in progress. Guitars and untrained voices float up to us.

We believe it is our last time together, and because we are sure we will never see each other again I discover terrors she has never confessed before. I learn now that not all her sounds during our loving are pleasure—that she is afraid, whatever our precautions, of pregnancy. And yet, she says, perhaps her fear is itself a pleasure, of a higher sort. I chide her for saying so.

"What else frightens you?" I whisper.

"Death," she tells me, "and dark houses, and being put away."

We cling drowsily to each other while the folksongs drift in through the narrow windows. She sings in my ear, so softly it is like hearing only her breathing wedded to melody.

> The snow is blowing in the street
> And my darling walks with the wind.
> Wait for me, my pretty girl;
> Let me catch up to your beauty.

I fall asleep imagining that she is her mother and I am her child. When I wake up she has already gone; the room is bright and silent.

She is a senior at a women's college in the East, and when we do meet after the summer—I have my own car by now, and I seem always to be tired because I have driven all night to be with her—the quality of our love has changed. We talk more, we are more self-conscious, we think we are wiser. Certainly we are more serious.

We sit in a diner just outside Philadelphia on the Main Line, talking about what we will do if a baby *should* come. She says she would have the operation, and see to it that I wasn't involved in the whole mess with the doctors and her father. I am horrified and offended. That is murder, I tell her, and I think neither of us wants that on our conscience. I say I think the best solution, if the problem ever confronts us, is for her to have the baby and give it out for adoption. I say it's all very well to argue that the child may be given out to unworthy parents, and his life made a mess, but I say that will be no affair of ours at so far a distance. I say I would do my best to pay for her having the child in some home or other, but she says that *if* it ever reached that point she would simply visit her roommate in Baltimore and have the child there. She tells me she has heard a bit about homes for unwed mothers, and she thinks her capacity for knitting, and reading *Time*, and watching morning television is limited. Neither of us ever uses the word "love" as we discuss this matter.

In the end, after we have finished breakfast and are having thirds on coffee, she cannot agree with my argument. Not that she disagrees with my notions about what murder is or isn't, but that she is incapable of giving in to the mechanics of my moralistic universe. Here is something we cannot share; it is as if she must embrace her fears. At best, we agree to look forward to some sort of cruel destiny; we need to be star-crossed lovers, to have the outside world intrude on us, like the law. So we invent crimes of passion, or daydream suicide pacts. Because we never exercise our imaginings to the limit it is unclear which of us is doomed to be done in by the other, or what is to be the method of our perishing in each other's arms. Without saying so, I think of her dark houses.

Just after Christmas we are snowbound at a motel on Long Island. For three days, between meals and love and hours wasted in front of the television, we look out the room's glass wall at the motionless parkway traffic. At breakfast on the day the roads are opened I ask her to marry me.

"Are you batty?" she says.

"I don't think so."

She finds a few strands of hair that have slipped out of the ribbon and twists them around her fingers. "I don't ever want babies," she says.

"Why not?" I ask, but she only shakes her head. I see I have upset her, that I have somehow threatened to emprison her. "You don't *have* to have babies," I say.

"That's why people get married," she says grimly.

I say no more.

We never quarrel in the ordinary sense of the word. Only now there happen between us long and recriminatory monologues which conclude more often than not in angry copulation. For a time we are incautious; it is as if we are threatening each other with the catastrophe of children. Jubilantly her letters tell me she is not pregnant, and we fall back into former habits.

Then she begins to smoke cigarettes. I want to punish her for that—for her lungs' sake, her voice's sake—but I can't think how. The dreams in her letters are frantic.

At the end of that hectic spring she graduates from her green and gold girls' school, and for the next ten years I neither see her nor hear her voice over a telephone. Letters still pass between us, but they are few enough and often months apart. Our lives take different directions—mine the ascendant but commonplace, hers the downward and painfully rare. My tedious graduate work ends at last; I survive my obligation to the army; I come back to live in the Midwest and work in electronics management. I have a satisfying life, a material freedom. If I have not said that I am married, let me say it—and there are children.

It is children—the two sons and the exquisite daughter—who most remind me of her during the long intervals between our letters, for I recall our dramatic talks in Philadelphia and remember how in that dim past there were days when I wanted her to conceive my child. I believe I wanted to frighten her, and by frightening her to strengthen my possession of her. I am ashamed of that memory now.

As for her, it seems to me that in these ten years—in letters from Paris, from Rome, from Geneva—she announces her engagement every six months, but never marries. In every city she finds a new teacher, and each stirs her to brighter declarations of her ambition for opera. But so far as I know she never gives a concert, never appears on a stage. Only twice does she touch on our time together. Once: "I liked the motels," she writes, "but after a while they weren't stagey enough." And the other time: "I think we had to admit—was the place called Avalon?—that it wasn't going to last. Love, or pleasure, or whatever *it* was. If you catch the hem of your coat in a car door, you can't trot alongside the car for the rest of your life, explaining your predicament to the driver. Sooner or later the car stops and the door opens and you're soaring free, or else you can't keep up, and the coat rips and you crash into the ditch."

I hoard her letters—for truth's sake—and then one day between summer and winter after a long silence the mail brings me an envelope addressed in her complex backhand script. There is no letter inside—only a hektograph program of a presentation by the patients of a state hospital in the East. Of course she is part of the program: she is to sing "The Snowstorm" and "Birches."

The drive—I have explained it to my wife as best I can—is a long and tiring one, reminiscent of those made in the past. I arrive on the eve of the performance, check into a motel near the hospital, sleep until the afternoon of the next day. When I ask the motel clerk for directions his answer is solemn—he supposes I am visiting a relative; perhaps he thinks I am tainted by that relative's illness, and he is sad for my uncertain future.

The hospital proper is a loose cluster of three- and four-storied buildings, some of red brick, others of yellow fieldstone. Over them, at a distance, towers a smokestack painted blue around its peak, letting into the sky a slow brown smoke. I see something of factory in this hospital, something of campus. Like a factory, the buildings are grimed and huddled toward a common product; like a campus, the architecture bridges Victorian and modern notions of institutionalism. Before each building is a wooden sign, black, with serifed gold lettering.

I park in the visitors' lot beside Administration. There are a dozen or so cars nearby; far off, up by the gate, sunlight glances off the windshield of the most recent arrival. By noticing it, I am trying not to think about my singer.

Administration is one of the older buildings. Two pairs of high double doors open into a lobby. The ceiling is whitewashed, and a row of light globes—like falling balloons—is suspended from brass chains over the center of the room. The walls are painted pale green and reflect the ceiling lights in shiny splashes that reveal brushstrokes. The floor is white—hexagonal tiles with black edges flowing away, through a further pair of doors, into a corridor unnecessarily large.

At my left is the information desk. It is a cheap-hotel arrangement, oak-fronted, with cubbyholes for mail mounted on the wall in back of the desk. Beside the mailboxes is a directory of hospital staff. A high clock reads ten before three in roman numerals. The performance is at three.

When I identify myself at the desk—to a sweet-mouthed, motherly woman—I am immediately directed across the main lobby to a large, cold room converted into an auditorium. No— into a concert hall. Folding chairs, five or six rows of them perhaps ten chairs wide, are set up facing a raised platform; at the rear of the platform: flags—the American flag at one side, the United Nations flag at the other. Thin swirls of vivid red and pale blue. A tall man in a green smock is just placing a white woven basket filled with carnations and gladioli: red and yellow and orchid-violet. A piece of worn oriental carpet has been put down to make a small rectangle of design near the front of the stage.

Fewer than twenty of us are in the audience. We are seated like so many strangers, far apart from one another, though off to my right I see one couple—perhaps a mother and father, holding desperate hands. I have chosen the third row. If I am not always a creature of habit, at least I am a creature of echoes and ghosts, or I would not have come to this place.

We wait. The cold sunlight slants into the room through a rank of narrow windows; hospital attendants move in and out, talking in low voices, pointing toward the stage, the light. After one such consultation a door near the front of the hall swings open and two men in coveralls wheel in an upright piano; they position it to the left of the platform. The piano is painted green, to match the walls. A moment later one of the men returns with a straight-backed chair and sets it before the keyboard. As the minutes pass, our restlessness in the hall is magnified by its near-emptiness—every creak and cough, every scrape of a foot resounds to the ceiling. I read and re-read the purple ink of the program, which is creased and dog-eared by my attentions and my impatience. Finally, at a quarter after three, the door at the front opens again and the performers file in—five of them—to take seats in the first row.

I recognize her at once, her long black hair still in a ponytail, her skin still startlingly white. Once seated, she turns and looks over her audience; she sees me, squints, waves discreetly. I return the wave. My hearbeat is like a drum inside my head.

I am not much taken by the entertainment—or I am so bent toward my singer, so concerned with how she may have changed in these ten years, that I have neither eye nor ear for anyone else. I am out of patience with the two girls who sing "Juanita," the plump boy who reads three poems by William Blake, the stately middle-aged woman who acts out bird-wristed passages from Louisa May Alcott. By the time the accompanist has at last resettled herself at the piano, my hands are sweating, my program is all but destroyed.

As before, the wait is justified. Even her step up to the platform is taken with assurance, with elegance. She is dressed plainly: bluejeans, a simple white blouse, loafers and white socks. For a few moments before she begins to sing she stands and surveys the sparse audience; she smiles at me—just the hint of a smile—and at a blonde, plaid-shirted young man I notice for the first time sitting in the second row at the left. Composed, she nods to the pianist.

This time it is "Birches" she sings first, wanting perhaps to end on the happier notes of "The Snowstorm," letting the sadness of "Birches" have only the briefest life in this place. Her voice is still a pure joy. If she seems somewhat heavier than I remember, then she has gained strength for its projection. If she is really ten years older, then age has made it wise. If she has continued to smoke cigarettes, she smokes little enough that it is not damaged. After all these years her Russian is flawless; mine has become a dead language, but hers would gladden dear Katerina Evgenevna as ever it did. It is foolish to say so, but I close my eyes and I am in love all over again. When the song ends, the applause is genuine and strong. I wish I were in a famous hall, in a famous city. I am eager for "The Snowstorm."

It begins well—the piano like the slow chords of a gypsy guitar, the singer's voice gentle, but growing braver in pleasure and praise.

> The snow is blowing in the street
> And my darling walks with the wind. . . .

Then she stops. The piano trails off. Her gaze is directed toward the rear of the hall.

Like the rest of the people here I turn to see where she is looking—a sensation much like fear clenching my stomach, as if I am afraid she is having an attack of . . . of what? Of whatever she is here for—loss of self? failure of future? All I see at the back of the room is what appears to be one of the hospital's doctors, a man about my own age, just now taking his place in the back row. The door through which he entered is clicking shut, the creak of floorboards is echoing in the bare room, his chair scrapes when he seats himself. He is the reason for her stopping; he is an interruption. The hall is electric with the new importance of silence. I wonder what will happen now if my chair squeaks, if someone coughs. I return my uneasy attention to the stage, where she has already calmed herself.

"I'm terribly sorry," she says in a disarming, shy voice. "Let me begin again."

And she does. And she is glorious. We forget the interruption, we forgive her curious sensitivity to the late arrival, we glory in her voice and her energy. The song is a triumph—more so than in the summer recital I hold so firmly in my memory— and I think the time between then and now need never have existed.

I am not the first of those who surround her after the program is ended, and I am pleased to see that the doctor whose entrance flustered her is among the ones pressing her with congratulations. The others are the patients who shared the stage with her, one of the men who wheeled in the piano, the youth in the plaid shirt. When she sees me nearby she separates herself from her admirers and holds out her arms to me.

"You," she says, "darling you—for not missing my debut." She laughs and hugs me, presses her damp cheek against mine.

"You're still terrific," I say. I am trembling, I know.

She takes my hand. "Here, I want you to meet this man." She stops me in front of the doctor. "This is Doctor English, who barged in late."

"Hello," I say. She seems not to be angry at him.

He pumps my hand. "I'm delighted you decided to visit. Isn't she a phenomenon?"

"She certainly is."

"Let me very quickly ask if you'd be willing to stay around for a few minutes at the end of visiting hours—just to exchange a word or two."

"All right."

"Good." He seems genuinely pleased. "Now I think you two old friends ought to go off and talk. See you."

I look at her. She has been standing a step or two behind me, one graceful hand twirling above my head as if she is casting a spell on me.

"It's a milkweed seed," she says. "Come on. We'll have a cup of coffee in the snack bar."

Again she takes my hand, and we walk together down the endless corridor, turning off it into the snack bar—a small, brilliantly lighted area crowded with chrome and plastic tables and chairs. It is about half filled with patients and guests; I see the young man in the plaid shirt sitting by himself in the furthest corner. He seems to be shadowing her.

"One of the things I think I'd like to be," she says as she

pours coffee into plastic cups, "is one of those enormous milk-weed plants with pods hanging all over them. Then at the end of summer I'd just burst open and scatter the seeds all over the countryside. Every seed would be a song." She hands me my cup. "Let's go over there," she says.

We sit as far from the others as we can, at a small table near the window where the autumn wind buffets the glass and the light of the sun waxes and wanes as the clouds cross. For all the years since we were so close, the years since I have seen her face, she is still lovely, with her exquisite pale skin, the deep, dark eyes, the delicious full mouth as distracting as it was when we were college lovers. But I see changes: she is indeed heavier now, the heaviness showing under her jaw and filling in the hollows beneath her cheekbones. Her hair is already showing streaks of gray above her forehead and at her temples. The light in her eyes is, if anything, brighter and wilder. She smiles at my staring—her smile like the sun, freed of the clouds—and lays her hand over mine.

"You're like an invited ghost," she says. "I feel as if I dreamed you, and when I woke up you'd gotten caught outside the dream and here you are."

I shake my head. "Still a dreamer," I say. I want her to see that I still love her after a fashion I could never explain, and that I want the mocking tone of our better past to be alive and lively.

"Well I'm glad you could be here for real. What did you think of the show?"

"You do sing as beautifully as ever."

"Thank you." She lowers her gaze; I sense she won't believe my compliments, so I resolve to offer no more. "I'm ashamed I got so spooky about Doctor English coming in late. Do you remember the songs?"

"Of course. You sang them that last summer."

"Today I sang them in memory of Katerina Evgenevna."

"Is she dead?" I have not heard, though even if the dear woman were alive she must certainly be in her eighties.

"Oh, yes." She looks thoughtful. "Don't ask me how I know. I think she may have visited me. Or I heard from somebody. I forget."

"She was a marvelous lady."

"Poor woman," she says. "She'd be horrified to know I've lost all the Russian I ever knew except the words to those songs."

"Oh, yes," I say, "so have I."

"But you're married now?"

"Yes. I got married a long time ago."

"And you have children?"

I nod; I wish she had not asked. "Yes. Three—two boys and a girl. The youngest just started kindergarten."

"Are you happy?"

"I think I am."

"So am I." She leans toward me, as if conspiring. "I have a lover here," she whispers. "He reminds me very much of you; I hope you're flattered."

I must look startled, for she puts both hands over mine and grips them, as if to arrest my reaction.

"No, it's all right," she says. "We're very careful. Very, very careful."

I make myself relax by fumbling for a cigarette. I offer one to her and she accepts it.

"I know," she says, "smoking is bad for the voice. But I don't overdo, really."

"That's good," I say. "Your voice is precious."

"His name is Barrett," she says. "He's good for me. We met in o.t., and we share the same psychologist."

"Is he musical?"

She gives me a curious look, then laughs. "My God," she says, "were *you?*"

A bell rings at the front of the snack bar. By the shuffle of feet and the general movement in the room I realize visiting hours are ended. I am both relieved and disappointed. We stand up together.

"That's Barrett," she says.

I look where she has gestured and see the plaid-shirted young man whose presence near her is constant. She flutters her fingers toward him and leads me out to the lobby.

"Is it a good marriage?" she asks me as we walk.

"I think so. As good as most marriages I know about."

She smiles. "I never gave us a chance. Sometimes I feel sorry; other times not."

"I know," I say.

"And you have your children after all." She puts her arms around my waist and hugs me. "There," she says, "we never were quite right for each other." She looks up at me and for the last time our faces are as close as years ago. Her eyes are underscored with blue shadows; her skin is coarser, the pores more open, the cheeks and brow flushed.

"They're good children," I say, as if they must be defended. Now we are in the main lobby; her shy young man has taken a seat near the mail desk. She stands on tiptoe to kiss my forehead.

"Thank you for journeying through time," she says. She gives me a second kiss. "Everything we can imagine comes true."

I tell the motherly woman at the desk that Doctor English has asked if he might talk to me. She uses the telephone to contact him, and in a couple of minutes I see him approaching me down the long corridor.

"I won't keep you," he says. "It's just that in the two years she's been here, you're the only person who's come to visit her. I wondered how well you knew her."

"Very well—once upon a time."

"How long since you've seen her?"

"Years. Nine or ten, I guess."

"What do you remember about her?"

"Everything."

"I mean especially."

I want to avoid his questions—at least tell him I think I ought not to be cross-examined about my past or hers—but I resolve to be polite. "Her dreams," I say. "And she refused to marry me."

He smiles wisely. "Her dreams are marvelous. Erotic as hell, but a remarkably complex eroticism. Highly structured. Her symbols seem mostly air-related."

"I know," I say. "Umbrellas, balloons—I remember."

He motions me toward one of the leather chairs across from the information desk. He sits facing me in a similar chair.

"Far more dense than umbrellas and balloons," he says. "And what's amazing is that she can draw them in detail after she's seen them in her sleep. Da Vinci would have adored her."

"What's wrong with her?"

"Hell, I wish I knew." He gives me a wry look. "Oh, the simple-minded answer is that she's manic depressive, but that doesn't say anything—and it might not even be 'wrong.' She's hard to get a fix on because she's so bright and talented. Cigarette?" I shake my head. "This was a really good day for her—I must confess I thought I'd shot her down by coming into the auditorium later than I'd planned—she's very *up*, high on the singing."

"It was always the most important thing in her life."

"Indeed. Her voice is just fantastic, though she does everything she can think of to wreck it." He waves his cigarette at me. "Smokes, of course. A couple of times has managed to get into locked cabinets and swallow things that might not kill her, but certainly make her throat raw. Screams at the floor attendants—I mean really abuses her voice beyond belief."

"Why?"

"Aha," English says. "Wish I could be certain. Did you know her parents? Or know much about them?"

"Just that her mother was a suicide. I used to think she blamed herself for that."

"Maybe. My feeling is that she blames her mother—not for taking her own life, but for rejecting her daughter by taking her life. She's not so hot about her father, either. Doesn't want children of her own, you know."

"Yes," I say, "we used to talk about that."

English looks rueful. "So do we."

"She told me she has a lover here. Is that possible?"

"That all she told you?"

"And that I shouldn't worry," I say. "That the two of them are being 'very careful'—I assume about not getting her pregnant."

He nods. "Yes, it's still much on her mind. And yes, it is possible—this not being a monastery. Barrett worships her, as you can probably tell by the way he hang-dogs after her wherever she goes."

"She says she met him here."

" 'Met' puts it mildly—but yes, he's not someone from her life pre-hospital." English puts out his cigarette and stands up. "Well, I think I'll leave you to your own world," he says. "I appreciate your staying."

"How *did* they meet?"

English hesitates. "Oddly," he says at last. "They were in an occupational therapy session—carpet weaving, or some such nonsense—and she went after him with a pair of shears."

I feel a chill. "She tried to kill him?"

He shrugs. "Hard to say if she was after his life or something else. In any case the therapist broke it up. I think Barrett was grateful for the attention—he's a withdrawn sort—and she surely felt guilty enough to do anything for him." He puts out his hand to me. "Really," he says, "I'm pleased—for her—that you could come to the concert. Forgive me for running, but I've got to wind up a few things before I can head home."

I shake his hand, unable to think of what else to ask him.

"Drive carefully," he says.

On my way to the parking lot I hear a tapping noise from behind and above me. When I look back I see her standing at a window on the second floor. Beside her, partly in shadow, is the image of a second face. She waves; I wave. Then I turn quickly away and resume my walk to the car. The other face is Barrett's, of course. I think how it might be mine.

Land Fishers

THE rain, which had fallen steadily for three days along the river and had begun a day earlier in the green hills to the north where the river took its source, stopped on Sunday morning. By noon the clouds had begun to break, blue sky appeared, and the sun—so much unseen through the long month of July— put down its warmth. The black trees turned green in the new light; their shapes, dull reflections on muddy water, flowed downstream; in the town parks beside the river dead branches eddied and turned, and the top rails of benches showed themselves. A single vast pool of slow water covered the town golf course.

The afternoon turned off hot, the air ponderous with the moisture it carried out of the flood. Smells which ought to have been drowned rose from the waters and lay like fog against the senses. A warm south wind moved across the leveled earth and through the sodden leaves.

"Venice might be like this," said Nora Swan, thinking of travelogues and Thomas Mann and the stories she had heard from friends who had been there. She was standing at the top step of the sunporch—the only dry step; a few inches lower the brown water began and stretched away from her. Over the lawn and the lawn furniture, twelve feet above the normal surface of the river and far across the opposite shore to the roadbed under the Illinois Central tracks which had carried no trains for two days. Venice. But here were no graceful gondolas, and no—

what did they call them?—no vaporettos. She could see some boats; not the usual powerboats with water-skiers foaming after them, but rowboats—neighbors plying the riverbank to inquire after friends, firemen ferrying aluminum urns of coffee upstream and to the river's two islands. The voices of the boaters came hollow across the water. One man—it was Paul Thorne, who lived at the far end of Cottage Row—waved to her, and she waved back.

"All right?" He cupped his hands around his face to ask; his dog, a Labrador pup, danced cautiously in the center of the boat.

"Yes," she called back, "all right." Her own dog, the dun-colored mongrel terrier Ray had nursed back from an automobile accident down the road, whimpered at her heels. "Swim out," she teased, but the dog shivered without moving.

The ringing of the telephone brought her inside, the mongrel limping after her to the kitchen at the back of the house.

"How is it?" asked her husband's voice. "How are you holding out?"

"Fine," she said. Looking out the kitchen window she saw the Jaguar sedan sitting on the back lot bonnet-deep in water. "The car's going to be a mess."

"How high is it?"

"Oh, Ray, I can't tell."

"Worse than spring a year ago?"

"I guess so. Or almost." The swing set they had never sold, even after the youngest boy had gone off to college, made wavy shapes on the water. "It's up to the hood of the Jag."

"How's the linoleum?"

"Fine. Dry." The linoleum was almost new, laid down in the spacious river-end of the downstairs after the Swans had put up for thirteen years—half their marriage—with a bare floor slowly going to warp and splinter. "Are you going to try to get home tonight?"

"I don't think so." Nora could hear him light a cigarette.

"The water's up a lot higher than it was when Tommy and I came in Friday morning. We're going to keep the room at the Holiday. Is that all right?"

"That's okay."

"Why don't you hail one of those firemen's patrol people and have them bring you downriver to the bridge? I could meet you with a cab."

"Oh— " Should she?

"What do you say?"

"No, I don't think so. I'll just stay and play water widow."

"Suit yourself," Ray said. "Do you need anything?"

"I'm pretty well off. I shopped Tuesday, and there's a ham in the freezer. If the power goes out, then I'll have somebody bring me in."

"Suit yourself, but it might be a long siege."

"How long are they saying?"

"Nobody knows for sure, but they're not expecting the crest until tomorrow forenoon."

"Then when will you be home?"

"I suppose I'll come back out on Tuesday or Wednesday with Tommy. But the road won't be open for another week—if the road's still usable, that is."

Nora twisted the phone cord around her fingers. "It's okay," she said. "I'll get along."

"Listen, I'll put in a call to Paul Thorne and have him stop in on you."

"No, I'll do that. He's still out on the river; I just talked to him—him and his Labrador."

"Right. Don't forget to rig up some kind of duty-box for Brownie. Use a bunch of old newspapers."

She turned toward the terrier, who thumped his tail. "I did. Do you have everything you need?"

"Almost. I picked up a toothbrush at Berg's, and I can borrow Tommy's shaving gear."

"I'll see you Tuesday."

"Or Wednesday. Here's a kiss."

The odd metallic affection momentarily amused her, and she returned it. Then she realized he was about to hang up. "Ray?" she said.

"Yes, what?"

"What will they do about mail?"

"I don't know. I'm damned sure they won't deliver it."

"All right. I'll have the television."

"Call Thorne's if you run out of anything."

"I will."

"Keep your feet dry."

"Yes. Behave yourself." He had already hung up.

By sunset the level of the brown water had come up more than halfway on the last riser of the porch steps. If it kept coming, relentless and silent, until tomorrow's predicted crest— well, there would be no help for the linoleum. No matter how deliberately she knelt inside the door, trying with tape and rolled-up bits of carpeting to seal the threshold, the river would enter like an unwelcome visitor; it would fan out across the shiny floor and encircle the legs of the piano, slide under sofas and armchairs, lap at the staircase leading to the second floor. She would have to abandon the kitchen—or slosh about in old overshoes to make meals for herself. Brownie would sprawl on the piano bench, confused and miserable. The Jaguar slowly sinking in the yard would smell for months like sewage and mildew.

"It's a price I'm willing to pay," Ray had said more than once. "Anything to be outside of town—all that fast-food crap, all that exhaust getting in your lungs."

She always agreed—only every two or three years this happened, the river out of its banks and possessions ruined. The usual season for it was spring, the Minnesota snows melting swiftly into the watercourses that fed the Turkey, the Cedar, the brown Iowa, and pushed them toward the Mississippi; once in a while, as now, remarkable rains flooded the summer—and here she was, solitary, while her husband stayed at a motel and carried on his classes at the university. Even when the children were at home, they too had stayed in town. She felt like jetsam; she felt like those New England sea-captains' wives who paced the cupolas of their square houses.

"Suppertime, Brownie," she said, and she put down the dog dish heaped with dry food. For herself, she was not hungry, but went into the living room to sit in the bay window with a skirt she was letting down, a few socks that needed mending, a linen pillowcase she had been embroidering for a niece who would marry in August. She worked listlessly—plying the needle for ten or fifteen minutes, then gazing out the window at a field of water she scarcely saw. When she realized the light had gone, she was startled and guilty. She heaped her work into the wicker basket and left it on the window-seat. In the kitchen she found a plastic container of fruit salad, left over from supper night before last, and ate it abstractedly, roaming about the downstairs in the dusk. When she decided to go upstairs to bed, it was not because she was tired, but because she could think of nothing else to do in her muggy prison.

Then, because of the emptiness of the house, the uncanny stillness lying like fog between the light of the half moon and the dark mirror of the flood, she feared she might not fall asleep without help. She arranged about herself on the bed an assortment of magazines—she had read them all before, their bindings had peeled away at the corners to show the discolored lines of their gluing—and on the stand beside the bed she set a half glass of water and a single yellow Valium tablet she had found at the back of the medicine chest. She was not sure the tranquilizer would put her to sleep, but while the children were at home Ray had never allowed sleeping pills—nor, for that matter, firearms or plastic bags from the cleaner's that she sometimes wished she could save, or even simple poisons to be used against nuisances like gophers and muskrats. So precautionary a man, his habits had become hers; sometimes, as now when she was alone, she felt the irony of diligently having preserved their sons from death by accident, and yet they were gone from her.

She took up the nearest magazine and held it unopened across her knees. The face on the cover was of a young woman— a girl, really—with dark eyes heavily made up and a mouth vivid with moist lipstick. Fashion. If she'd had daughters, would they look like this girl, eyes wiser than their ages, lips glistening like tomato flesh? Inside the magazine more young women appeared, even the wholesome ones fabricated from bottles and jars—polished, burnished. Nature looked arranged for them.

She laid the magazine aside and got up to turn on the television set on the dresser. Then she sat, propped against pillows and feeling like a queer kind of invalid, through the ten o'clock news; Brownie lay against her legs. The flood was featured. The reporters—Lord, they were so young—drifted up and down the river with microphones outstretched, the camera's eye taking in silent streets whose dark waters lapped at ranch house window-sills, rowboats of volunteers weighty with the desire to rescue the city, farm animals forlorn on tiny islands of pasture. Then— there—just for a moment her own riverbank home passed across the screen, herself nowhere to be seen, as if she had already fled to higher ground or perhaps gone under the brown tide unnoticed and unmourned.

She switched off the set as soon as the weather report was finished, and took the Valium. The sports segment held no interest for her—not since the high school days of their older son, a basketball center, when they had put up a backboard beside the house. She remembered the day she and Ray had brought it home from the sporting goods store near the college, how carefully they had hidden it behind the shed under an old tarpaulin, how they had persuaded both boys to dig a hole for the support pole by pretending they were going to put in a yard light. The pole still stood—a four-inch pipe whose bright orange rustproof-ing had long ago faded and begun to peel; the backboard had been sold two years ago. It was eerie how the evidences of happy memories were incomplete, how parts of the past were always missing so that even if it were possible to go back in time you could never reconstruct the life you lived there.

She did not know how long she had been asleep when something woke her, and still more time passed—in silence, her breath held—before she realized what had disturbed her. The bedroom was remarkably light; the brightness of the moon was a clear, hard aura along the edges of the window-frames. Brownie, permitted to sleep at the foot of the bed only when Raymond was away, had also waked. He lay rigid against her legs, head up, ears stiffened, curiously like the pets buried with ancient kings—and exactly as effective. Noise. Nora sat up and reached for the lamp beside her; she felt the switch snap under her fingers, but no light came. Power outage. She fumbled in the drawer of the nightstand, found the flashlight, and swung her legs out of bed without turning the flashlight on. The dog remained frozen.

Nora did not let herself be frightened. It was true that the noise seemed to be coming from inside the house, downstairs, but she might be deceived. She knew enough of flood times to realize how the world of sound could change. Carried across the extraordinary reflector of high water, things far off seemed close; small noises magnified themselves. What she had heard might be hundreds of yards away. Then, too, she had no way of knowing how much the river might have risen since her bedtime; if the engineers had been mistaken about the time of the crest and it had come early—if it were already inside the house— she might have heard some floating object. Perhaps the water was so high that the downstairs furniture was sailing into the walls; that would make this the worst flood ever.

She got up and started for the stairs—still holding the dark flashlight. "Stay put, Brownie," she whispered, certain of his obedience.

Halfway down the stairs she heard the refrigerator door close. She felt a sharp thrill of fear in her stomach. Dear God, she thought, and her mind danced through explanations: Ray had changed his mind, he had asked Paul Thorne to meet him at the First Street bridge and bring him out to the house—but there was no power; he would have come upstairs for the flashlight if he wanted to raid the refrigerator. Or it was a neighbor, another wife—perhaps Tommy's—who, like her, was stranded and alone and had paddled over for companionship—probably she had neglected to lock the back door, for who would come wading through all that water?—and that made a kind of sense. Perhaps it wasn't the refrigerator at all, but the screen door coming closed. Or—and this was in and out of her head as swiftly as a dance of light—one of the boys was home from college, had decided to surprise her, was ravenous the way sons always are. How muddled she was. Valium. The odd suspension between asleep and awake.

"Who's there?" she said.

Silence. Then whispers. Had Ray brought Tommy home with him?

"Is it you, Ray?"

Someone was walking toward the stairway; the beam of light from an electric lantern dazzled her.

"It isn't Ray," a man's voice said. "It isn't nobody you know of, I don't believe."

It was a young voice, not threatening.

"What do you want?" she said.

"What have you got?" An older voice, rougher. "You come the rest of the way downstairs and be sociable."

She descended, stood at the foot of the staircase with her right hand resting on the railing. The flashlight—she had not once turned it on—was in her left hand.

"We didn't think people was in the house," the young man said. "We truly didn't."

"Are you burglars?"

"I guess."

"We're fishermen," the older man said. "Only we're fishing on land because all the fish are drowned."

The lantern light danced at her feet; in the shadows it made she watched the shapes of the two men, wondered what they might do with her in this empty house on the swollen river.

"I don't have any money," she said.

"We'll take anything we can catch. You keep a gun in the house?"

"No. We don't believe in guns."

"Who's 'we'?"

"Raymond—my husband and I."

"He upstairs?"

"He isn't home. He's staying in town until the river goes down."

"You ought to've gone with him," the young man said. He was the taller of the two; the paleness of his face in the indirect light suggested to Nora that the other man might be bearded.

"I suppose I should." The light brushed her face and she turned her head away. "Don't shine it in my eyes," she said.

"You sure there's no guns?"

"I told you we don't believe in them." Or knives; anything. Once one of the boys had come home with a slingshot and Ray had confiscated that, too.

"Neither do we," said the young man. "Except for duck hunting."

"Close your dumb mouth," his partner said. He raised the lantern and surveyed the room they were standing in.

"What are you going to do?" Now that she knew the intruders had no weapons, Nora wondered if she might persuade them to leave. Then should she phone the police? But if she charged trespassing, the men would say that they were lost on the water, that they were only looking for a refuge until daylight.

"You don't have no money?" the older man said. "You don't keep nothing valuable? Jewelry? Silver?"

"No." It was almost the truth. She had her engagement ring, and of course the wedding band—surely they wouldn't steal those from her—and there was the cultured pearl necklace in the small drawer of the dresser, but everything else was junk. Some things—a plastic bracelet, two or three inexpensive pins and brooches the boys gave her—of sentimental value. And the silver—a place setting for eight they had used only once: Ray had put that in a safety deposit box when the prices jumped. "No, nothing that would interest you." Her older son's stamp collection; she had forgotten that.

"What's your old man do?"

"He teaches."

The older man cursed softly. "You sure as hell pick the winners," he said.

"We aren't very well-off," Nora said.

The beam of lantern light played around the living room. "Stereo," the older man said. "Piano. You're not so damned poor." He reached over and took the flashlight out of her hand. He gave it to the boy in exchange for the lantern.

"You use the torch and get the Mrs. here out of the house for a while. Give her a boat ride. I'm going to do some more looking-around."

"It's true," Nora said, "there isn't anything worth taking."

"We'll see."

The young man grasped her wrist and drew her down the last two steps. "Come on," he said. "It's a warm night out there."

She held back.

"Nobody's going to hurt you none," he insisted.

She let herself be dragged after him. When her bare feet touched the floor she felt the wet layer of river cool on the surface of the linoleum. Oh, damn, she thought, and in just that instant she was more concerned for the house than for herself.

The young man opened the front door; water rippled around it like whispers.

"Watch yourself," the older man told him. "Don't get lost."

The boat was a small one, moored to the heavier branches of the lilac tree outside the door. The young man helped her into the boat—for a moment she was fearful he was going to push her, make her fall, but almost at once she realized his clumsiness had mostly to do with his trying to be careful about touching her. Respecting her. He had rested the flashlight on a seat so that its light broke over the ribs of the boat, and helped her over the gunwale by holding her wrist and guiding her with his other hand at her waist.

"You sit back there," he said. "I'll be in the middle, facing at you."

She sat. The wood under her was warm, as if it still held the heat of the sun from hours earlier, but her feet were cool from the wetness of the living room floor. She could imagine what would happen inside the house while she was out of it—the water rising slowly, that man sloshing through the downstairs, tracking dirty water up to the bedrooms, his muddy hands on clothes and toilet articles and the porcelain handles of the dressers—and then she remembered the dog.

"Brownie," she said.

The boy paused at the bow, stopped untying the rope at the lilac. "Pardon me?"

"The dog. I have a dog—named Brownie. He's upstairs."

"Jesus," the boy said. He vaulted onto the steps, water splashing in the faint light of the moon like bright flowers.

"No," she said, "he won't hurt anybody. He's just a sissy mutt."

"What am I supposed to do?"

"Get him—he's in the big bedroom." She wondered if it was smart to bring Brownie to the rowboat. "No—shut him in the bathroom," she said.

"He won't bite?"

"No," she said. "He'll be too scared even to bark."

She sat, feeling sorry for poor Brownie, and took stock of the situation, of herself. Here I am, alone in a flood, drifting in a rowboat in my front yard, while two strangers rob my house. Now what? Where would this polite young boy take her while his father—surely that was his father—ransacked? A boat ride under the half moon. Venice. Perhaps he would sing to her, or she to him. While she was thinking of him, he reappeared at the front door and finished releasing the boat from the lilac.

"I did what you said—stuck him the bathroom. He was shaking like a leaf."

"He's not much of a watchdog."

"What do you keep him for? He a good hunter?"

"No."

"He's kind of a little kid's dog. You got little kids?" He pushed the boat away from the steps, stroked once with the oars and let the slow current take the boat.

"I used to. They're big kids now."

"They off at school?"

"Yes."

"I went to school for a year—tech school. I was going to be a mechanic, but I ended up just a gas-pump jockey."

"You quit the school?"

"Money," he said. His face was in shadow; she could see the hitch to his shoulders when he said the word.

"That's too bad," Nora said. She meant it. Seated in the stern of the boat, feeling the humid warm night on her face and arms, seeing the long shadows the moonlight made of poplar and cottonwood, she thought of her own sons—how fortunate their lives had been, how she wished this young man had stayed in school, become skillful, learned a better life.

"You want a smoke?"

"Thank you. I don't smoke."

"I mostly don't," he said, and then instead of lighting a

cigarette he put the pack in his shirt pocket and returned both hands to the oars. "It's weird—all the water."

"It is."

"It filled up our basement yesterday morning—put out the pilot in the water heater."

"It makes a mess of things," Nora agreed.

He let the boat drift. The bow turned slowly downstream, the stern coming around so she could look back at the house that was almost luminous under the moon. If they went on in this direction they would come to the bridge where Ray had wanted to meet her; perhaps if she thought hard enough he would leave the Holiday Inn and drive to the bridge—"I don't know what came over me; I just felt this urge to get to the bridge."—and the boy whose captive she was would steer without knowing why to the landing where her husband waited.

"I wonder why you do this?" she said. "This stealing."

"I don't know." His voice was soft, shy. "It's not a good time for us—for me and Dad. It didn't seem like a bad idea, to take some things. We wouldn't hurt nobody."

"No," she said. "I know you wouldn't."

"And we'd never've come inside your place if we'd known you was there. We steered clear of any place that showed a light. We figured if a house was dark, then probably the people stayed in town because of the flooding."

"The power was off."

"But we didn't know that, see. We thought the place was deserted. We even rowed around the whole house to look things over."

"Yes," she said, "I understand."

"That's a foreign car, isn't it? The one behind your house?"

"It's British, a Jaguar."

"That's a fancy make."

"It's only about seventeen years old," Nora said. "Almost as old as you are."

The boy laughed. "Really," he said.

She tried to study his face, though the half moon was too soft on his features for her to see details, and just when she thought she was seeing him whole—a strong jaw with just the slightest handsome cleft in it, a straight nose, a lock of hair careless on his forehead—the shadows of one or another tree limb crossed the light and broke her attentiveness. He must be very close to the age of her younger son.

"How old are you?" she persisted.

"Nineteen," he said. "Twenty next month."

"My youngest son was born in August, too," she said. "But he's a couple of years older." She sat with her hands folded in her lap, a pose that reminded her how little she was wearing, how vulnerable she was—if a forty-six-year-old woman could be said to be vulnerable before a nineteen-year-old child. "Where are you pumping gas?" she said.

"Right now, nowhere. The guy who runs the station, he told me to take a couple months off. His volume is way down."

"What does your father do?"

"He works in the foundry at John Deere's—when he works. He's laid off, too."

"I'm sorry."

"Misery's got company," the boy said. "I bet most of the people we know are laid off. It isn't so awful."

"But if it makes you a thief—" She had no idea what she had started to say, but it must have been something obvious—or condescending—and she could not close the sentence.

"Look," the boy said, "are you sure you don't want a smoke? It isn't an ordinary cigarette; I got it off a kid I know. It makes you feel really nice."

"Is it marijuana?"

"It's not sprayed with chemicals or anything. It won't make you get sick; I've tried it."

"I don't think so." She realized she was smiling—a grown-up's smile that said she understood without needing to share—

and she remembered the one time she had smoked part of a marijuana cigarette with Raymond. "But you go ahead."

"You won't mind?"

"No, I won't mind."

She watched him in the dim light sort through the cigarette package until he found the joint, watched him while he lighted it—the boat drifting in a lazy spiral around one dipped oar—and took a long draw from it. The concentration amazed her whenever she watched someone inhaling marijuana—dope, pot, whatever they called it now. ("You can't waste it," Ray had said. "You have to get all the good out of an expensive habit.") She could imagine the boy a hollow figure, and the heavy blue smoke spreading through him until he was filled—and then he would exhale.

"It's nice," he said. "You really should try it once."

"My son had a stash when he was in high school. One time his father and I smoked a little of it."

"He find out?"

"I don't think so. We never told him."

"My dad would be real upset."

"I won't tell on you. Honestly." And when he offered her the cigarette she accepted it and brought it to her lips.

"My mother's dead," the boy said.

She did not respond, but passed the joint back to him and sat holding her breath, thinking: What does he want me to say? Is there something I'm supposed to do? How long did his father tell him to keep me away from the house? The smoke felt like feathers in her lungs—a vague, not unpleasant irritation that she thought might turn into a cough—and she began to hear the blood in her ears hammering dully. She felt like stretching her arms, and did. Then, when she thought she could hold her breath no longer, she counted to ten and let the smoke out into the moonlit night.

"Feel anything?" the boy said.

"Just out of breath." She took a great gulp of air. "Do you have brothers and sisters?"

"No."

"Do you have pets?" Oh, God, she thought, listen to me babble.

"We got a dog about as brave as yours," he said. He sucked at the cigarette and returned it to her.

"It's nice to have something to talk to when you're alone," she said. This time the smoke was not feathers, but moisture—a mist inside her that she could feel gathering on the branches and twigs of her lungs, as if she were a tree unleaving, the leaves growing from the water they absorbed. She felt uprooted, turning slowly over and over through the night. She exhaled, choked, felt her eyes tear.

"You okay?" The boy took the joint; she watched its small orange brightening.

"Floating," she said.

After a few moments he said, "That's because you're in a boat."

"Yes." She giggled. "In a boat, you float."

She held out her hand to the boy; he drew her across the space between them until she was sitting beside him, her free arm around his shoulders. What is happening? she thought. What is happening? But nothing happened. The boy did not kiss her, nor she him; she brought his head to rest on her bare shoulder and held him, gently, the giddiness from the drug obliging her to close her eyes. It was as if Nora Swan were living up to the name her husband had brought to her—as if she were the graceful water bird drifting, stately, over the slow surface of the river. That she might now fly—bow forward over the moonlit waters and kiss goodbye to the earth with a last light touch of white breast-feathers while her long wings drummed the air—seemed as possible as this curious reality. Clinging to the boy, the boat revolving her idly in the flood, she felt less than stolen from, more than loved; the solitude of her days seemed sensible, almost bearable. What would she do, she wondered, if this boy touched her? She let herself imagine such a thing: his hand—it would be rough from his work on automobiles—perhaps touching her breasts, lightly, as if he were unsure of himself; perhaps once—just the once—bowing against her, putting aside the bodice of her nightgown to kiss her. Would it be like mothering? or would it be a violation of the sort she had imagined as she stood on the dark stairs? and when she said, "No. Please, no," would he catch the small regret under the foolish flood of her emotions?

So, finally, nothing serious bound them. The boy was neither child nor lover, and she had clung to him, her bare arms around his neck and shoulders, only to keep herself from floating into the sunrise like milkweed. She returned to her place in the stern of the boat and sat quietly while the boy rowed against the current. The sky beyond the trees along the riverbank turned bright with morning; Nora guessed it must be after three o'clock. She felt tired, the muscles of her back and arms ached as if she had been doing some difficult physical work. Yet she had only gone for a boat ride and shared with a young stranger a drugged cigarette—and this was not Mann's Venice after all. Tension. It was tension that made her ache, and the uncertainties of the night.

"I hope you're taking me home," she said.

The boy smiled, nodded. "My dad's going to be wondering."

She hugged herself. In the light, she thought again how little she wore—how exposed to him she had been all along.

"I won't tell about the cigarette," she said. Then she wondered if she would tell Raymond. And if she did, would he be angry at her, suspicious of her imaginings, her wishes? Would he chastise her and remind her she was old enough to know better? Or would he—as she had done all her adult life—would he be so relieved she had come through this perilous experience unharmed that he would say nothing unkind, but only embrace her and say: "Thank God you're all right."

She watched the boy's face as he plied the oars. Now she could see him plain; she could see how much more coarse he was than her own sons, as if the simple opportunity for going away to school was refining and smoothing. But perhaps it softens as well, she thought, and perhaps my children have too much to learn about the hardness of life—that it is not only for the privileged, that there are some it takes from, and those taken from survive the better.

The sky was pale yellow and the tree limbs bowed into the bright surface of the flood. The home she shared with Raymond came into view, framed by the dead elm on the far side, by the poplars on the near. It rose out of the nearly motionless water like a painting—the brush-stroked art on the walls, perhaps, of Ray's motel room: under the shade of lilac branches the sun-porch windows reflected, foreshortened, the peak of the roof catching the earliest sunlight. She tried to imagine what might be happening beyond the blankness of the windows, the real windows. She wondered if this young man's father was finished with the house, with opening drawers and cupboards and look-ing for valuables like a relative after a funeral. She thought of how she would spend the rest of the day—cleaning up: not only the water that had spread over the new linoleum and brought mud into the corners of the downstairs rooms, but where the father had been. His fingerprints. His footprints. Perhaps the odor of him, like grease, or the ozone of the factory that had laid him off.

"Back the same day," she said.

The boy nodded. He shipped the oars and let the boat slide silently across the front yard toward the steps he had led her down only a few hours earlier. The river was receding; the top step was already dry.

"Hope there's nothing here for me to run aground on," the boy said.

She thought. The bricks for the barbecue grill they had never gotten around to building were piled at the side of the house; the mound of dirt Raymond had brought in, intending to recruit the boys to level the lawn, had overgrown into a landscape and showed as a tiny island above the water's surface.

"No," she said. "You're safe."

Now she could see something inside the house—a face, unfamiliar, dark-bearded, nearly God-like. It moved from the window nearest her, gliding, a pale presence against the dark interior, toward the door.

"You'll likely hear some bad words," the boy said. He let the bow bump against a step, grind alongside it. "Catch a hold on one of those branches."

Nora caught at the lilac and felt the weight of the boat tug at her shoulder muscles. Above her, the door swung open and the father emerged. He carried the lantern that had first blinded her on the stairs, but his other hand was empty. She supposed he had gathered together the things he intended to steal, heaping them near the door while he waited for his son.

"Jesus H.," he said. "I didn't ask you to spend the night in town."

"We lost track of the time," the boy said.

"I bet," the father said.

"And the river's going down. The current's harder to make headway against."

The father came down one step and held the screen door open. In the daylight he seemed to Nora neither menacing nor dirty—he looked rather like one of the men who drove out from town once a month to read the meters.

"You can have your house back, Mrs.," he said.

"You got stuff to load?"

The man shot a scornful look at his son. "I said you sure as hell can pick winners. I'd sooner steal from the poor house." He helped Nora out of the boat and up the steps.

"Thank you," she said.

"Don't bother," the man said. "If I'd seen anything worth stealing, I'd have stole it."

"But I'm grateful, really."

He stepped into the boat. "Your dog's still in the john upstairs. If you're going to be out here alone, you ought to get yourself a German Shepherd or something."

"Brownie's just company," she said.

"We got a worthless mutt ourselves. That's what my old lady used to say: 'just company.' " He gestured at the boy; the stern of the boat swung slowly away from the steps. The man touched two fingers to the side of his head. "Nice meeting you," he said.

She wanted to thank him again, but knew how foolish it would be—a woman in a flimsy nightgown, standing in her doorway to shower thanks on two men who had threatened to rob her, had frightened her with the prospect of being hurt, perhaps raped. Yet for an instant she found herself trying to think of a way to show them her gratitude—by finding something of value she could coax them to steal? or by offering to make them breakfast? She thought of the canned ham she had bought for Easter before she had realized her sons would be absent and there was no point to a fancy dinner; she could give them that.

But they were already fifty yards away and moving out into the current at the heart of the river, a solitary boat on the diminishing flood, soon to be misty with distance. Venice. A foreign place. A language she hardly knew. She felt all manner of sensations: the chill of what might have been; the marvelous absurdity of her leaning toward this child boatman; the pure and blessed relief of the end of uncertainty and—deepest by far—the paradoxical fact of all her possessions intact about her.

Thalia

I T begins with me sitting in one of the luncheonette booths at
the Dollar Store. I'm fiddling with the menu, slipping out
the Special for Today from under the celluloid to see what they
covered up, when in walk Candace and her sister. Both of them
are dressed summery, her in a pink-and-white stripey dress thin
enough to show off the whole shape of her legs when she comes
in the door with the sun behind her, and her sister Thalia, who is
seventeen and ought to know better (or if she doesn't she ought
to be told some things), wearing a white tee-shirt and Levi's.
Both of them have on white tennies, and Thalia's got a pink
ribbon tied around her head over the top of her hair. She's a
brunette and Candace is a blonde, and you couldn't imagine two
girls more different from each other.

They come straight over to the booth and stand looking at
me. It's like Candace wants to punch me in the eye the way she
looks, but Thalia is all serene.

"Hi, Candy," I say. "Hi, Thalia."

"I want words with you," Candace says to me. "Go try on
hair ribbons," she tells Thalia, and Thalia drifts off to the back of
the store somewhere.

"What's up?" I ask Candace, and I move my feet so she can
sit across the table from me.

"I'm up," she says, "right on the ceiling I hit yesterday
midnight."

Candace and me are engaged, and we're planning to set the

date very soon—maybe in a couple of months, because the 'dozer man is threatening to walk out on old man Powers and if they move me off the truck over to the 'dozer then I'll be making enough money to afford to get married. Lately Candace has been very touchy about everything. I guess she realizes pretty soon she'll be chasing the moths out of her hope chest.

"What's the gripe?" I say. I sit straight so as to look concerned about what she is saying, and I try to make "What's the gripe?" sound serious and sympathetic.

"I suppose you don't remember last night," she says.

"Of course I remember last night," I say. "It wasn't so long ago I'd of forgot it already."

"Then why do you ask?" she says. She takes a cigarette out of my pack in front of me, and the way she taps it on the table before she puts it in her mouth looks like she's driving a stake with it.

"I remember you didn't come to the party," I say. "Is that what?"

"Is that all you remember, Sweets?"

"It's some of it," I say. Candace almost always calls me *Sweets*, and I call her *Candy*, which would sound sickening after a while to somebody listening, though that's none of their business. "I'd of remembered if you *did* come, too," I say.

"I was at the telephone company late," she says. "I called you and left you a message with your boss, if you want to know."

"As it happens, I was dumping gravel in a man's driveway who lives on the other side of town," I tell her. "I went straight home without going back to check for any personal calls at my answering service." I don't notice if she catches my being sarcastic because just then I see Thalia, who has got sick of the ribbon counter and is floating down to the front of the store and looking over a shelf of goldfishes in little bowls.

"It seems to me," Candace says, "that when someone finds he is in mixed company where alcoholic beverages are being served, and his fiancée whom he expected to be there isn't there, then he should do the proper thing and politely excuse himself from the guests and leave that company."

"And it seems to me," I say right back, "that if the said fiancée feels like voting prohibition on her husband-to-be against alcoholic beverages, then she ought to think again. I'm nearly twenty-two," I say, "and I'm still foot-loose and free for a while longer."

I see how she looks a little sheepish, but at the same time I'm watching over her right shoulder how Thalia is stooped over the goldfish counter with her face up close to one of the bowls. She is playing games with the fishes, opening and closing her mouth like she was breathing under water. It's like she's going to kiss the glass, and I wonder what the goldfishes are thinking. I know what I'm thinking.

"It's not the alcohol for itself," Candace goes on, "but what it does when it gets inside of you."

"I don't see that what happens inside of me is under your control," I tell her. Thalia is tucking in the flap of her tee-shirt where it's worked out of her Levi's at the waist in front. It makes me think of the health spa ads on television, and I have a taste in my mouth like it was full of sugar or honey. Thalia is a really grown-up seventeen, if I didn't mention it already.

"What includes my sister *is*," Candace says. She goes all soft the way she looks at me, and she puts out her hand that wears the cameo ring I gave her from the carnival last year, and she takes hold of my wrist. At first she has hold of my watch-band, but then she moves her hand and hangs onto my wrist.

"Oh, Sweets," she says, whiney, "how could you do that while I'm working hard at the telephone company, earning money so we can get ourselves off to a good start in marriage?"

The kind of work she does down at the telephone company is that she is a long-distance operator; she is the one you get when you call collect, and she listens to you recite your name and your number and then she says "Thank you." She doesn't even have to dial the call for you. She just has to tell you her operator number and then say "Thank you." That's the kind of back-breaking work she's having a fit about in the Dollar Store.

"Come off it, Candy," I say. "If it was Thalia told you things about last night, then it's probably all lies anyway."

She pulls her hand back and sits stiff as cement. "That is a *deliberate* falsehood," she says. Icicles.

"I *beg* your pardon," I say. This is sarcasm again, and Candace knows it.

"It so happens I saw with my own two eyes," she says.

"And what did your own two eyes see?" I come back.

"I expect you don't remember that vacant lot at the end of Maple where it runs into Hickory."

"I expect I do remember that vacant lot," I say. "I walk past it every time I come to pick you up for a date and every time I bring you back from having it."

"Then you know what I'm talking about," she says.

"No, I don't," I say, "and I wish you would be plain."

"If you want to know—" She stops, like she doesn't want to say what she's going to. "I saw *you* in that vacant lot."

I keep my mouth shut, wanting to find out exactly where I am in this discussion.

"I saw you," she repeats. I think she may be getting hysterical, her voice is so different from a telephone operator's. "I saw your big, bare posterior-part, up above that tall grass like . . . like two melons." I don't say anything. "The street lamp was lighted, and I could see all the way from the sidewalk where just anybody could have seen you in that . . . that obscene position."

Needless to say, people all over the store are looking funny in our direction, so I say to Candace: "Well, listen, why don't I call the manager over and ask him would he mind having a sign printed up about it, and he could tape it to the mirror behind the lunch counter next to the Coke-and-sandwich posters so everybody could read it while they're eating?" A guy could get a reputation.

"You don't deny it?" Candace says.

"I'd certainly like to know what makes you think the particular fanny you saw belonged to me. It's not like being face-to-face."

"Well, when I come home from working at the telephone company until after midnight, and I find you missing from the party and Thalia missing, too, then I don't need any IBM computer to put two and two together, do I?" she yells at me.

"All right," I say to her, "you think what you want, why don't you?" In all the hollering and with Candace making such a spectacle of herself and starting to cry, I've lost track of Thalia. She's not teasing the goldfishes any more. Then I pick her up again by the candy cases, and right while I'm watching I see her reach in and swipe a handful of caramels off the top shelf of the case nearest the door. The clerk is up at the other end of the counter, weighing fudge for a little old lady, and Thalia just snakes out to the street like a neurotic dancer and is gone.

"She's only seventeen," Candace is saying, meaning Thalia.

"She's no baby," I say. "You can just bet she knows what's right from what's wrong."

This sets her off again. "My God, you're not even ashamed!" she blubbers at me, and then she puts out her cigarette in the ash-dish like a hot poker in somebody's eye, and she slides out of the booth and sails off.

"Wait a second, Candy," I say. We've had *discussions* before, and I'm pretty sure I can make things all right. This time she doesn't answer me. She just stops inside the door at the crippled kids gum ball machine and sticks in a penny she's dug out of her purse. Then she stalks back to me and she drops this pink gum ball on the table in front of me. It sounds like a shot when it hits, and I catch it from rolling off onto the floor.

"That's the only kind of candy you'll get from here on," she says, and she's out the door.

I pop the gum into my mouth and go on sitting in the booth for a while, thinking how I'm still probably going to get that promotion, and how Candace maybe wasn't right for me after all. Then I go out and stand on the sidewalk in front of the Dollar Store, and after looking both ways to see if Thalia is anywhere in sight I pitch the gum out in the gutter and take off to the arcade on Sycamore where the guys usually hang out. It doesn't take so long any more to suck the sweet out of a gum ball.

An Inward Generation

1. *Meadow Green, 1939*

A T sunset the boy sat at the foot of a slender pine tree, watching out across the meadow, motionless and mute as stone. He sat tensely, weight balanced on his arms, his coveralled legs angled away from his body and crossed at the ankles. A cover of pine needles lay under and around him; his hands were wrist-deep in the cool spills. He seemed almost not to be breathing. The evening wind brushed past him and went on to stir the meadow grasses and the black foliage of the apple orchard beyond. Blackbirds swept out of the trees in the direction of darkness. The boy stayed, staring across the dusk at something he had never seen, until his head ached and tears came to the corners of his eyes.

He had arrived at the meadow early in the afternoon, running up the long, dusty hill overlooking the town, catching at spires of goldenrod and crushing the pollen in his hands until his palms were cobwebs of yellow. Behind the tumbled stone walls along the way the fields bled wild roses, and the maples were already insisting autumn among the evergreens. Far below him the town was a mosaic of dollhouses, toothpick shrubs, the sparkle of tiny autos. The orchard was at the crest of the hill; the meadow stretched beyond it and commanded the world. To the west, black and purple hills gave way to distant white mountains. To the east was the cold gray edge of ocean. South were the yellow blueberry plains, and north through the pine groves lay uncountable lakes. Here the boy could be himself; on this sandy soil that held stiff grasses rasping against his hands he paced off his giant-steps of independence. No one crossed him; no voice called him home. No adult had ever interfered with the satisfaction of solitude.

Today was different.

Today he had come to the meadow, passing under and through the fragments of orchard sunlight, whistling and talking to himself. Ahead of him he kicked at the shriveled windfalls. In his hands he carried a branch from a wild rosebush and stripped the thorns from the stem with his fingers, rubbing it smooth as he went on. By the wall of loose stones laid between orchard and meadow he paused—and it was then he saw the other two.

They were walking toward him slowly, a man and a woman hand in hand, intent on each other. The boy dropped the rose branch and hid quickly behind the wall to watch them, peering through a crevice where the stones parted. They had not seen him. As they came closer he prayed silently that they would not discover his hiding place; he also prayed for them to go away.

When they were not far from him they stopped and sat down among the spare, tall grasses. He could hear them talking, but he was not close enough to understand the words; they talked for a long time. The man was dark-haired, but the woman was blonde with tanned arms and legs and curious bright eyes the boy could see because she faced him. Then the two of them kissed. The boy realized something was beginning; he thought he must have realized it when he first saw them, or he would not have stayed, hidden, afraid of being found out.

The woman wore a pale blouse, then no blouse, and a moment after the upper part of her body was naked. The boy held his breath. In the afternoon's clarity she seemed unreal, perfect, and he was splendidly surprised. He watched her lie back against the earth, saw the man touch her lightly, bend to kiss her mouth. Then the man lay beside her and put his lips over her breasts, one and the other, where dark pigments like wild roses melted in circles. She held the man's head with her thin hands; the boy thought he heard her cry out. He was suddenly frightened, crouched behind his wall, wondering if she had seen him through the narrow crevice. Fear and guilt tightened his stomach; he wanted to run through the orchard until he had reached the dusty road and left the meadow behind. But much more, he wanted to see, and after minutes of fearful waiting when he heard no sound he moved back to his spying place.

Now both of them were naked, lying together in the disturbed grass, the woman's golden body half concealed by the whiteness of the man's. Their clothes were strewn about them. The boy knelt with his fingers pressed hard to the coarse rocks of the wall, until the rocks began to sweat. He drew his hands away and put them to his face; his fingers and palms were moist, his cheeks chalk dry.

The man and the woman became the measure of time. Their shapes blended and parted. Now they were curiously twined, like bleached tree roots; now they were separate, poised apart. The boy saw no reason for this. He saw the man's hands move smoothly everywhere, memorizing his partner's body, and he saw the woman cling to the man, her own hands leaving marks of petal color on his skin. He waited. The man drew away, leaning back against his heels like a swimmer resting on a beach. His fingers touched the woman, then slipped forgetfully away to the ground. They were talking again, the words lost in the wind and leaves. The man bowed to kiss her eyes; he was like a shadow that hid her from the boy.

And then he ran away—as fast as he had ever run in his life, head down, fists clenched—but not toward the road leading to town. Instead he stayed in sight of the old wall that divided orchard from meadow, and when after a while he stopped, out of breath, he crossed the wall and backtracked and sat down in the grass. It was late; the sun was below the horizon and the sky to the east was a rising purple cloud. He thought the world had taunted him with some marvelous prize, holding it just beyond his reach, and now the prize was getting further and further away—more distant than it had been at first in the weak cry of the woman kissed.

He got up and walked across the meadow, head down, heels scuffing the sandy ground. When he reached the carpet of pine needles in the silent grove he went down on his hands and knees and crawled, lifting his head every few yards to look out across the darkening field. Finally he saw the man and woman. They were walking away from him, vague shapes in the dusk, their movement blurred by distance. But even if the man and woman had been invisible he could not have forgotten all he had seen. In a few moments they were out of sight; the meadow belonged to him. He walked through the brittle stems of the meadow until he reached the place where they had lain and he had watched. The grass was flattened; they had left nothing behind. The boy lay face down where the lovers had been, weeping for his ignorance.

2. Business, 1947

"OKAY, now here's the way it works. You all set?"

"Yes, sir."

Mr. Osborn pushed a yellow pencil into the corner of his mouth and looked up from the books. Monty, the manager, was standing across the room beside the filing cabinets, talking to the new clerk. Mr. Osborn listened.

"We got a big business here, you understand, and it takes a lot of paper work to keep big business straight. We got to have efficiency, right?"

"Yes, sir."

"Okay. Dunlap's is the biggest auto repair outfit in the world, almost, so don't forget that."

"No, sir."

Mr. Osborn showed interest around the end of the pencil. The clerk was a youngster, eighteen or nineteen. The job paid thirty-five dollars a week.

"We fix a lot of cars in here, maybe sixty, seventy a day. That means paper work." Monty opened one of the cabinets and took out a sheet of paper. He waved it at the boy. "You see this? This is a copy of the statement we send the customer. There's four copies. There's white; that goes to the customer. There's pink, there's yellow, and there's blue. The blue one goes to the bookkeepers. The pink and yellow is where you come in."

"Yes, sir."

"You got all that? White, pink, yellow, blue? White to the customer and all the rest of it?"

"Yes, sir."

"Okay. First thing you do is this: You take the pink sheet and you check this file here." Monty slapped the top of one of the cabinets. "Then you find the little white card with the customer's name on it. The same name as on the pink sheet. Then you copy down three things on the little card: the date, what was done on the car, and how much it cost. You got all that?"

Mr. Osborn chewed his pencil.

"Yes, sir."

"Now," Monty went on, "if there ain't any little card with the customer's name on it, you make one out." He patted a small cardboard box on top of the cabinet. "The blank ones are right in here. You make it out just like the cards already filled in. Customer's name and address, model of the car and when he bought it; and then the date, what work was done, and how much it cost. You got that?"

The boy nodded; in back of his eyes flickered an expression of heavy pain. Mr. Osborn pinched his lip thoughtfully and looked back at the ledger opened in front of him.

"Okay," Monty said, "now after you got that done, you file the pink and the yellow sheets in these drawers. The pink ones on this side, the yellow ones on that side. You file 'em alphabetically, A-B-C, last name first. The yellow with the yellow, the pink with the pink. You sure you got all that?"

"Yes, sir."

"That's all there is to it; just don't get behind. You got three filing cabinets, two big ones and a little one, and that's all you got to worry about. Cards with cards, pink with pink, yellow with yellow. Alphabetically, A-B-C, last name first. That's all you got to remember. And sweep up the office at five o'clock every day and be here in the morning at eight sharp."

"Yes, sir."

"You might as well meet the guys that work here." He led the boy to Mr. Osborn's desk. "This is Osborn."

Mr. Osborn looked up, smiling, and held out his hand. "Hi," he said.

"Jim Baxter," said the boy.

"Happy to know you, Jimmy."

"You see there?" Monty said, pointing to Mr. Osborn's desk, "he's copying the blue slip into that ledger."

The boy gave Monty an odd look. "Right," he answered.

Monty scowled. "Okay, okay, I just thought you might want to know what else goes on around here." He gestured toward a man seated at the desk behind Mr. Osborn's. "This is Pastorino."

"Pleased to meet you, Mr. Pastorino."

"Huh." Pastorino waved without looking up.

"You better get started," Monty said. "We been minus a file clerk almost a week and a half; things are kind of piled up."

"Sure."

"Go out through the shop." Monty pointed beyond the row of narrow windows separating the office from the cavernous garage. The garage was filled with glistening autos and the blunt noise of hammers. "All the back copies we stacked up on the table in that little room on the left. Grab a handful at a time till you get caught up. Okay?"

"Okay," said the boy.

"Okay," echoed the manager, and he slapped the boy on the shoulder. "You got any further questions?"

"When do I get paid?"

"Week from Friday." Monty grinned at him. "It's got to work that way, you understand. Gives the boys in payroll a chance to check your time card."

Jimmy nodded without returning the grin.

"It's all yours," Monty said.

Jimmy opened the door into the shop and went out. Mr. Osborn glanced a question at the manager.

"Another dumb kid," Monty said wearily. "I give him a month." He sat down at his desk, across from Mr. Osborn's.

"I think he needs money."

Monty shrugged. "That's why he's working." He took a thin black cigar from his shirt pocket, lit it and studied the burning tip. "You understand," he said, "that's why everybody works."

Mr. Osborn tapped the bow of his glasses with the yellow pencil. Jimmy came back into the office, carrying a sheaf of pink and yellow papers. He went to the filing cabinets and slid open one of the drawers.

"Pink with pink," Monty said pointedly. "Yellow with yellow."

At five minutes to twelve Mr. Osborn finished copying a stack of blue statements into the ledger and laid the yellow pencil neatly on the desk in front of him. He turned in his seat.

"When you going out to lunch, Patsy?"

Pastorino frowned vaguely at Mr. Osborn. "Go ahead," he said finally. "I'll eat the late shift."

"That's the ticket," Mr. Osborn said happily. He stood up buttoning his vest and pulled his jacket down from a hook on the wall above his chair. He put on the jacket and looked around the office. Monty had already left with the shop foreman; silence filled the twilight of the garage. The new boy was slouched over his filing cabinets, tucking pink and yellow papers into the steel drawers, humming softly to himself. Mr. Osborn watched him for a long moment.

"How about a bite of lunch, old scout?"

Jimmy looked up and stopped humming.

"There's a dandy little cafeteria down the block." Mr. Osborn took a short step toward the boy. "Darned good food. Pretty reasonable, too."

The boy appeared to be thinking it over. "Sure," he said. "Sure, that sounds like a good idea," and he put the rest of his papers on top of the cabinet.

"Let's go, scout." He said it briskly. "Got to be back at the mines in an hour flat."

Jimmy held the front door and the two of them went into the street. They walked side by side, neither of them saying a word. Then Mr. Osborn put his finger to the tip of his nose and scratched tentatively.

"Can't beat New York in June," he said.

"Nice and warm."

Mr. Osborn cast a sidelong glance at Jimmy. "No, sir," he insisted, "you just can't beat it."

"I hope this place is pretty cheap," the boy said.

"Very reasonable. Very popular. They do a big business with low prices on the menu. Volume, if you know what I mean."

"Yeh."

"It's part of a big dairy outfit. A national chain." Mr. Osborn stopped walking. "Right here. Started out as an employees' cafeteria, but everybody in the neighborhood eats here. You know how these things get started."

They went into the cafeteria through swinging glass doors trimmed with bars of chrome. Inside was the sound of voices over the rattle of plastic dishes, the smell of cigarette smoke mingled with the odors of the steam table. Mr. Osborn and the boy stood with metal trays and followed the line to the cash register. The girl at the register wore a yellow apron, and stood with her hands on her hips while Jimmy fumbled with a handful of small change. Her streaked blond hair was stuffed into a hair net, and her face seemed incapable of a smile.

"They just hire the ones who can make change," Mr. Osborn said as they crossed the tiled floor to a table. "They don't get paid to be cheerful. That right, Jimmy?"

The boy didn't answer.

They sat at a corner table, emptied the trays and put them on another table across the aisle. Mr. Osborn looked at the boy over his sandwich.

"How do you like it?" he asked. "The new job."

"All right."

"What do you think of Monty?"

The boy raised an eyebrow. "Is he as dumb as he talks?"

Mr. Osborn snickered. "Monty's all right at heart, old scout. A little hard to get to, that's all."

Jimmy nodded and gulped his coffee.

"Where you from?"

"Maine. Town you never heard of."

"How long in New York?"

"Three days." The boy studied Mr. Osborn. "How about you?"

"That's the ticket," Mr. Osborn said cheerily. "Remind the old man how old he really is."

"I just wondered," Jimmy said.

"Forty years," Mr. Osborn said. "Loved every minute of it. Wonderful place, New York."

The boy shrugged. "For you, I guess. I haven't been here long enough."

"You'll like it. A wonderful place."

"Sure. I already like Grand Central Station."

"How's that?"

"I've slept there the last two nights." The boy looked proud. "At least I tried to sleep there."

"Just like in storybooks. That right?" Mr. Osborn winked.

"Like in the movies."

"How much cash you got with you?"

"All I've got left is twenty-eight cents."

"Where you going to sleep tonight?"

"Same place, I guess."

Mr. Osborn reached across the narrow table and curled his fingers around Jimmy's wrist. He squeezed it reassuringly.

"Stick with me, old scout. We'll get you all straightened around."

"I don't get paid for ten more days. That's not even three cents a day." The boy disengaged his wrist.

"Stick with me." Mr. Osborn wiped his mouth with his fingers. "We'll show you where the city's heart is."

"Sure," said Jimmy.

The two of them got up from the table and threaded their way to the glass doors. On the street, walking back to Dunlap's, the boy asked:

"What's Mr. Pastorino like?"

"Patsy? Salt of the earth. Oh, he's not easy to get acquainted with, but once you get him warmed up he's the salt of the earth." Mr. Osborn paused outside the door of the office. "You'll see."

Inside, Monty had already returned from lunch and sat smoking a cigar, his elbows on the desk. Pastorino was putting on his coat. Mr. Osborn clapped his hands together and began to talk hurriedly in a loud voice.

"Monty? Patsy? What say we take up a little collection for Jimmy here, just to help him out till payday? He's got no place to stay, no money—" He faltered for an instant. "I figured if each of us kicked in four bucks apiece, Jimmy could pay us back next Friday and have himself a place to stay in the meantime." He looked from one to the other. "What do you think?"

"Four bucks?" Pastorino seemed stunned by the amount.

"Just until next Friday. What have you got to lose?" He turned to Jimmy. "You could get by on twelve bucks, couldn't you?"

"It would sure help."

"How about it, boys?"

Monty took out his wallet and thumbed through some bills. "Why not?" he said. "Friday's fine." He looked at Jimmy, then back at his money. "But only till Friday."

"That's the ticket," said Mr. Osborn, and he took the money from the manager. "How about you, Patsy?"

"Okay." Patsy fished a handful of paper money from a trouser pocket. "Four bucks for a place to stay."

"And four from me." Mr. Osborn handed the bills to Jimmy. "What'd I tell you?"

"I'll see you around two," Pastorino said. He left the office without looking back.

Monty crossed the room to the shop door. "Don't blow it on booze," he warned, and went out to the garage.

"You're all set, Jimmy, old scout." Mr. Osborn slapped the boy on the back. "You stick with me after work tonight and we'll set you up with a room where I stay. It's real cheap, and you meet a lot of nice people."

Jimmy stood in the center of a solemn silence, crumpling the money in his hand. "Thank you," he said. "I didn't expect this."

Mr. Osborn hung up his coat and sat before the opened ledger on his desk. "You better get busy," he said carelessly. "You got plenty of time to thank me." He reached for the yellow pencil, dropped it on the floor and awkwardly picked it up as the boy went back to work.

Soon after five o'clock Mr. Osborn and Jimmy made their way along Fifty-Sixth Street off Eighth Avenue. The older man was a few paces ahead, waving his arms as he talked.

"It's right where that sign is, up ahead." He pointed. "It's what's called a residence club." He grinned back at the boy. "I lived here fifteen years myself. That's what I call a residence."

"It's a long time," the boy said.

A few yards before they reached the club Mr. Osborn turned an abrupt left and led the way through a narrow entrance, up a short flight of steps into a hall. On the left was a closed door; beside the door was a cardboard sign:

ATLAS SCHOOL OF ART

Beneath this sign was another, smaller one, hand-lettered:

LIVE MODEL
Wednesday and Friday
General admission Two Dollars

"This is really the back door," said Mr. Osborn, not stopping. "But it's closer to the desk. I'll show you."

He led Jimmy to the right into a low-ceilinged, smoky lobby. At the back of the room were grimy windows that looked out on a fire-escape ladder and the rear of another building. Scattered about the floor were leather armchairs and swaybacked leather couches, most of them brown and all of them cracked with age. The ceiling was supported by fat pillars; at the base of one of them was a greenish brass cuspidor.

"Come on," said Mr. Osborn, and he motioned Jimmy to the other end of the lobby. At another doorway he stopped and pointed. "This is the front door."

Jimmy looked down a short flight of steps to the street entrance. He nodded.

"Come on," said Mr. Osborn, "let's meet Mr. Hughes."

On the way back Jimmy was looking at the other side of the lobby. A pair of dusty windows overlooked Fifty-Sixth, and between the windows sat two old men playing checkers. The desk was placed at a right angle to the front of the building, and behind it were several rows of pigeon-holes for mail. A tall, gray-haired man stood behind the desk, pondering a puzzle in a book of crosswords opened in front of him.

"Mr. Hughes," said Mr. Osborn, "I'd like you to meet a friend of mine, Mr. James Baxter. Jimmy, this is Mr. Hughes."

"How do you do," the boy said.

"Haya." Mr. Hughes scratched his cheek with a soiled finger-nail.

"Jimmy's only been in town a few days, and he hasn't scouted up a place to stay yet. I'm helping him get his bearings. You got a room here, Mr. Hughes?"

Mr. Hughes pushed his book aside.

"Eight-fifty a week." He tilted his head at Jimmy. "In advance."

Jimmy winced. Mr. Osborn wrinkled his eyes into a smile and patted the boy on the shoulder.

"That's all right, Jimmy. We'll stretch out that food money okay. Don't you worry, old scout." He turned back to the man at the desk. "It's a good room?"

"Seven-oh-eight. On the airshaft, just like yours."

"That's the ticket, Jimmy; you get to see the sky. Go ahead and pay him."

Jimmy paid and put the receipt in his jacket pocket with the room key.

"Come on," said Mr. Osborn, "I'll show you where it is," and he hustled Jimmy once more into the back hall. He stopped before the skeletal door of an elevator. "Pretty nice for a dump like this, hah? It runs all the time, except when Sal's asleep. Sal's the guy runs the elevator."

"Seven-oh-eight," said Jimmy. "That's the seventh floor."

"You bet," said Mr. Osborn. "A long walk up if he's asleep, but he's usually awake till midnight, anyway." He stepped back and studied the dial above the door. "Sal's on his way down. It's a slow car."

"I left my bag in a locker at the station," the boy said. "I have to get it pretty soon."

"That's the ticket," Mr. Osborn said. "As soon as you see your room."

A frame of light appeared; the metal bars slid aside. Sal was a little bald man with a puffy nose; he looked like a dwarf.

"Here we are," said Mr. Osborn. He stepped into the car, Jimmy trailing. "This is Jimmy Baxter. He's up on seven."

The car started rising, whirring and creaking.

"Sal's a little deaf," Mr. Osborn confided. He leaned over the man and bellowed in his ear: "I'm getting off at five! This guy," pointing at Jimmy, "goes to seven!"

The dwarf nodded without looking up.

"You have to know Sal," Mr. Osborn said. "Once he warms up to you, he's the greatest guy in the world."

The elevator stopped at five. Sal opened the door and Mr. Osborn stepped into the hall. "You go on up and take a look at your room and find the gents'," he told Jimmy. "I'll meet you in the lobby in ten minutes. We'll make some plans."

The door slid shut and Mr. Osborn walked briskly down the dark hallway to his room. He opened the door, closed it behind him, and turned on the light to disperse the tall-building gloom. It was a small room with an iron bed against one wall and a dresser against the other. In front of the single window was a caned chair. The light bulb hung from the ceiling, shielded with a small pink shade. Mr. Osborn took off his jacket and threw it on the bed, then he stood in front of the mirror above the dresser and stretched his arms over his head.

"Another day," he said out loud.

He leaned closer to the mirror and squinted into it. What he saw was a thin, wiry little man in his late fifties, with a head of unruly white hair that needed cutting and overlapped the bows of his glasses. Mr. Osborn inspected a threadbare spot on his vest, scraped at a tiny pimple in the corner of his mouth and took a step backward.

"We'll have a cheap Italian supper," he told the glass, "and then take a walk around the town. He ought to like that."

He put on his coat, turned out the light and made certain the door was locked. On his way to the elevator he stopped in the men's room and came out whistling. The dial indicated that Sal was on the ground floor. Mr. Osborn used the stairs.

In the lobby he found Jimmy standing over the checker game. He gripped the boy's arm.

"What about an Italian supper, old scout?" he said. "A five minute walk around the corner?"

"I have to get my bag," Jimmy said.

"That's the ticket. A nice long walk to get the appetite up." He tried to lead the boy to the door. "Let's get started."

Jimmy hesitated. "I'd rather go alone," he said.

"Long way to carry a bag all by yourself."

"It's not very big. I thought I'd get a hamburger on the way back."

Mr. Osborn shuffled his feet. "You're the boss," he said. "How's the room?"

"Fine." The boy started toward the front entrance. "How about if I see you here in an hour?"

"Okay," said Mr. Osborn. "Any time at all."

"I'll see you later."

Mr. Osborn sauntered over to one of the leather armchairs and sat down slowly, folding his hands in his lap. He crossed his legs and began whistling very softly to himself, waiting for the hour to pass.

"What I'm saying is this," Monty insisted in an angry voice. "It's just what I told you from the first day that kid walked into the office and stood around like King Solomon or somebody. He's another punk who doesn't know what it's all about, I told you. Give him a month and he'll be out on his ear. I told you that."

Mr. Osborn pushed the eraser of the yellow pencil hard into his palm and shifted uneasily in his chair. "I don't know, Monty," he said. "If you'd give him a chance—just half a chance."

Monty leaned over the desk. "A month, I said. Okay, so I over-estimated the kid and he only lasts six days. Okay. I made a mistake. But I was right when I said he was just another dumb punk who wouldn't last. You got to admit that."

"But he gets the work done, Monty."

"Okay, he gets the work done, but how does he do it?" Monty straightened up. "I'll tell you how the hell he does it. He does it like he's some kind of genius or something, like the job's beneath his dignity. That's how he does his work, and that's just the way I don't want it done."

"Maybe it's too easy for him." Mr. Osborn sank deeper into his chair. "I don't know, Monty. So help me, I don't."

"You know where he is now? I'll tell you where he is. He's out in the shop, watching guys straighten fenders." Monty snorted. "He's more interested in what *they're* doing than he is in what *he's* supposed to be doing. That's not the kind of people I want working for me. You got a job in my office, you do the job you're paid to do. And that's all. Anything else, you can do on your own time."

"I think you ought to give the boy a break." Mr. Osborn snapped the pencil point against the desk. "Listen, Monty; Jimmy's had a rough time of it. No money, new in town, no friends. You got to consider that. I been doing the best I can to help him out, but it takes time for a youngster to work himself into things, don't it?"

"Wait till I talk to that guy at the employment agency," Monty said. "Three blanks in a row he's shot at me."

"Monty, listen. I'm the only real friend that kid's got. Let me talk to him, man to man. Maybe I can straighten him out; he'll listen to me, and I know darned well he'll take some good old-fashioned advice from a guy that's got his best interests at heart. How about it?"

"I already got his check down from Payroll. If the kid can't figure things out for himself, I don't want anything to do with him." Monty opened the door to the garage. "You! Baxter!" he called. "Come in here." He turned back to Mr. Osborn. "And you remember one thing," he said. "I still run this office—not you and your odd-ball buddies."

Mr. Osborn took another pencil out of the desk drawer. "I just thought you were being a little hasty," he said softly.

uncertainly over the man. "Thanks a lot for everything," he said. "I've got to get that bus home."

"You're wrong, Jimmy." His voice sank. "You're making the mistake, old scout."

He sat back with his elbows on the table and stroked his lower lip with a damp forefinger. A waiter came over and began to gather up the glasses and milk cartons. Mr. Osborn watched him clear the table.

"Too bad about him," he said muddily. He chuckled at the waiter. "Scared, I guess. New York scared him."

He lifted his elbows while the waiter wiped the table with a damp rag that left little beads of moisture in its wake. Mr. Osborn pinched his lip.

"It never scared me," he said. The sound of his own voice surprised him.

"You want something from the bar?" the waiter said.

Mr. Osborn looked up. The waiter had turned around to wipe a nearby table. "No," he said to the waiter's back. "No, I was just leaving."

He was aware of laughter, the clink of glassware, a taxi horn in the traffic outside. He stood up and buttoned his vest.

3. War Games, 1952

IN 1942, when I was a child, the walls of my bedroom looked like the inside of a recruiting office. On one wall was an enormous National Geographic map of Europe, with black and red pins deployed on it to represent the armies of Germany and Russia. Nearby I had tacked up a full-sheet color photograph of Douglas MacArthur, from the Sunday pages of the Boston *Post*. All around the room, high up near the ceiling, I had arranged fifteen or twenty pictures in full color of American and British warplanes, clipped from a magazine called *Air Trails*. And in

the closets where I kept my toys were regiments of lead soldiers, squadrons of wooden airplanes, and cast-iron armadas of
every imaginable class of naval vessel. That was my romantic
time. It was a pleasure to watch the swastikas and rising suns
proliferating over the AP newsmaps in all the papers—a pleasure because I (and Righteousness and Democracy) was only
biding my time, letting the enemy eat to the last slender half-
inch of the maps, before I wheeled savagely and made him spit it
all back. When the politicians said "our boys," they meant me, I
thought, and all the neighborhood kids I played at war with, and
all the long, tall daydreams that took me off to sleep at night
cast each of us in the parts of generals cocky at the points of our
armies, and admirals faultless on the bridges of our flagships. It
was ten years later before the romantic and the real crossed
paths for me, when I was at Camp Kilmer, New Jersey, waiting
to be shipped to Germany.

In 1952 nothing was like my old, fond dreams. I was only a
two-striper; there was no real war in Europe (though Korea was
on, and I hoped the worst); we were no vast army, but only a
respectable measure of replacement. Nothing was like the war-
dreams, but it was a beginning, and it was a time when "our boys"
included me, actually, and a few friends, actually, and one
eighteen-year-old private named Don Bradley.

Waiting at Kilmer was an exercise in patience, for the military has a talent for making waste and monotony into a way of
life as correct and formal as if it ought to *be* a way of life. As a
barracks unit, as a lawn-mowing detail; in ragged lines, in neat
formations; in card games, in bull sessions; at attention, at
ease—we simply waited.

Each morning's muster presented the only stimulus to the
clever man; either one avoided duty for the day, or one didn't.
Muster was held, after breakfast, in a great grassless meadow.
We were hundreds of men learning how great was our capacity
for waiting—rank on rank, file on file, army and air force en-

listed men standing at rest while an officer read at us from a wooden platform. First we heard the names of the men ready to be shipped, envying them as they dropped out and jogged off to collect their gear. Then we listened to the miscellaneous announcements. And finally we were arrived at the reading of the duty assignments—numbers of men required—while a sunburnt NCO went about the business of selecting the men to fill the rosters.

His selections were random. Sometimes he chose by files, sometimes by ranks; sometimes he picked consecutive rows, sometimes he skipped. It was no system to be analyzed, only to be guessed. Every man was on his own, and the olive mass of fatigue uniforms in the meadow became a shifting, sliding sea of individuals playing the shirker's game. We stepped back, stepped ahead, sidestepped—into any one of the gaps left by those who had been alerted for shipment. The object was to stay one move ahead of the duty sergeant; sometimes we outguessed ourselves and walked squarely into his web. It was a pitiful exercise in tactics; it was our war games.

No detail was ever difficult, of course. We policed the barracks areas, trimmed the colonel's hedges, counted linens (sheets and pillowcases in an army never wear out from being slept on, only from being counted in supply rooms), emptied trash baskets, and once—once I outsmarted myself onto the prison detail.

Prison detail was glorious, and only three of us were chosen for it that day. We put on the class B uniform, with garrison cap, and reported to the stockade, a sprawling yellow structure behind a high, wire fence. There we separated, and I will never know if my two comrades had for themselves so satisfying a day as I had. I was given an armband designating me as a military policeman. I was issued a carbine. I was even allowed a clip that held three rounds of live ammunition.

Live ammunition may not mean much to an infantryman, but I was a corporal in the air force. I had spent weeks in basic training, marching up and down narrow streets with an empty carbine on my shoulder. I had spent days falling in a field of crushed rock onto my knees and elbows, holding an empty carbine in my hands. I had spent hours being taught to take the carbine apart and put it back together again. I had come to love the stubby little carbine, .30-cal., M-1; it was my weapon, and if real war ever visited me the carbine was to save my life.

All that devotion was in order. I had responded to my training like a model recruit. Yet at the end of it all I had fired my weapon exactly fifty times, and I had done it on a range, under someone else's rules. I had borne the humiliation of collecting my ammunition five rounds at a time as if I could not be trusted with more, and I had been threatened with court-martial if I tried to steal a single cartridge. I had done all my firing with a non-commissioned officer at my ear, mumbling me advice, trifling with the placement of my elbows. I had submitted to the long-winded ritual of the firing range, starting from "Ball ammunition lock and load," and temporizing its way to "Commence firing." Then I had ten seconds to squeeze off my precious five rounds and begin the whole ceremony over again. Ten tiny seconds to indulge the freedom of shooting my carbine.

So the prison detail was a glorious event.

I was given a real prisoner to escort across the camp to a dreary clapboard building where his court-martial was to be convened. I was instructed to follow the prisoner with my carbine at the ready. I was authorized, if he tried to escape, to order his halt, then to fire a shot over his head, and then to shoot at the fleeing prisoner himself—low and in the legs, if possible. The responsibility was so wonderful, I was nearly dizzy with it.

It was my prisoner who was named Don Bradley. He was a slight, crewcut youngster with a narrow, squirrely face, and he wore, every time I looked at him, a quite innocent smile. Two days earlier he had got drunk in the barracks, walloped an old army tech sergeant behind the ear with a bottle, and cursed at the MP officer who came eventually to arrest him. It was a slight enough crime, and from the few words we exchanged he seemed really not a bad kid. If he had known how my mind would rebuild him, he might never have smiled.

We set out, Bradley walking a few feet ahead of me with his arms loose at his sides, setting the pace, knowing where he was going. I came after, walking pompously, the butt of the carbine poised against my hip (I couldn't decide whether the butt should ride just above or just below the sharp corner of the pelvic bone, so the poise was a wavering one), terribly conscious of myself, my mission, the armband I wore. Before we had gone fifty paces I had entirely transformed this boy, giving him a low, sloping brow, yellow teeth, cruel eyes—a street-gang delinquent whose parole officer had given him a choice between joining up or going back to reform school. Worse (better) than that, I had rehearsed my response if Bradley should try to escape, and I had it meticulously worked out so that the instant he made his break I would simultaneously drop to one knee, cry "Halt!" and fire the shot in the air. The next moment I would have him in my sights and bring him down, cleanly, with a bullet in the back of the neck. Finally I would slip the third cartridge out of the clip and hide it in my shoe. My imagined explanation to the investigating authorities indicated that I had fired, generously, two warning shots, and I honestly had meant to hit him low.

For the mile I escorted Bradley, my mind danced through this performance a hundred times, and I heartily wished for him to make his lunge toward liberty. He didn't; I considered shooting him anyway, but fought it. We both arrived unscathed at the judge advocate's office, and twenty minutes later, when we started back to the stockade, I felt my blood-lust once more boil up without boiling over. I didn't hear Bradley's sentence, but the military code, I knew, dealt severely with indecorum and disrespect, and I could expect that his punishment was adequate even though it had not been for me to impose it. I could at least pretend that it was my superior soldier's discipline which had earned me temporary control over a man's life. What I salvaged from my errand was that feeling of pride, of a sense that I had at last done something genuinely military—and a nearness to the conditions and tools of war which was never again permitted me in the four years of my service.

It wasn't long before my name turned up at the muster formation, and less than a month later I was in Bremerhaven, at the army staging area, awaiting final assignment in southern Germany. It was October, cold and bone-damp, with horizontal blades of rain hacking at the old airplane hangars and the neat brick barracks buildings. I had escaped to the service club, and one of the hostesses had sat down to join me in a game of cribbage. I happened to be facing the entrance, and all at once I caught a glimpse of that narrow, squirrely face wearing its innocent smile.

Bradley saw me at once. He came grinning over to shake my hand, and the hostess, assuming we were long-lost friends, moved away to let us talk. It turned out that it was not the parole officer, but the courts-martial board that had given Bradley his choice—sixty days in the stockade, with forfeitures, or immediate assignment to Berlin.

I remember how my dignity was staggered, and all the abstract salvages of my childhood took a severe lacing. For an instant I wished I had put that ball into the back of his neck after all, but I see now I had my first clear, sharp insight into the several things that have to be understood about "our boys" and the evenhandedness of war.

4. The Cause, 1962

TATE MORGAN had never tried to justify the amount of time he spent waiting for the daily mail delivery, either to himself or to his wife. He only knew that he *did* wait for it, and that no day of the week was truly begun until the postman's truck had driven by and he had walked out to the box to bring back whatever was there.

"Anything?" his wife would say as he pushed the kitchen door closed behind him.

And Tate, who had sorted through the envelopes and papers on his way up the driveway, would shake his head.

"Junk," he would say.

"Bills?"

"Not even that." Then he dropped the circulars and the magazines on the kitchen table and went down to his study to grade the student papers he should have been working on for a couple of hours. Once in a while he went to work on a small poem, for it was the small poems coming back that he mostly waited for in the mail. Now and then the small poems did not come back; instead there would be a note accepting one and telling him that his payment was a year's subscription to a small magazine, and thereafter he could look forward to *that*.

Sometimes, rarely, he went to work in his study before the arrival of the mail truck, but then he kept an FM radio playing softly behind him, and when the truck was within a block of his box he could hear its engine sparking against the radio's music. He would trot upstairs and hang around the living room window to see the mail truck turn the corner into his street.

"Stop pacing," his wife would say.

"You'd think that idiot could sort his mail at the post office," Tate would answer. "He's been shuffling letters at the end of the block for a half-hour."

Sundays and holidays were a great desert in his life.

He tried to time his weekdays so that he got up just before the mail came, at around ten o'clock. In this way he managed to miss the quibbling that surrounded breakfast and getting the children off to school. At nine-thirty he got out of bed, dressed, made his own breakfast, and brought in the flyers and the arty magazines.

One unusual Monday morning Tate overslept the delivery;

his wife brought the mail into the bedroom and sat on the edge of the bed. Tate opened his eyes.

"Anything?" he said.

"Three copies of *Silver Falconer*, and one copy of the *Crabwise Review*."

"Uh-huh." He closed his eyes.

"And a letter from Athens."

He sat up. "Greece?"

"Georgia."

"Must be from old Jerry Carl." He opened the letter and took out a sheet of onionskin paper. On it were three dense, typewritten paragraphs, with a list of names following. Tate looked to the bottom of the list and found the names of Jerry and Bev Carl.

"Yeh, it's from the Carls," he said.

"What is it?"

"Some kind of chain letter." He read it aloud. It outlined a plan to buy a bus for taking Southern voters to the polls. " 'Within four days,' " Tate read, " 'please send ten trading stamps of any kind to the person whose name appears at the top of the list below.' " He glanced at the names that headed the list—a couple living in Wisconsin. He looked down the rest of the list: another Wisconsin, a Florida, a New York, and the Carls.

He finished reading. There was an address, and some initials—SNCC—that barely made sense to him.

"Read that part again," said his wife, "about how many stamps."

He read: " 'Within 27 days you should receive 37,000 trading stamps, enough to fill 20 books.' "

"My God," his wife said. "Are you going to throw it away?"

"Of course not. It's a good cause, isn't it?"

He got dressed and carried a sandwich downstairs to his study. He took out of his typewriter the first three and a half lines of a small poem and made five copies of the letter, pounding like hammers the keys of his portable and adding his and his wife's names to the list, just under the Carls.

Then he began making sample lists of the five people he would send the letters to. He didn't want to pass them all on to his colleagues at the university; they would perhaps do the same, and the inbreeding would make a mess of the plan. It occurred to Tate as he was trying out names that 37,000 stamps meant 3700 letters. That excited him.

When he had finished sifting his prospects, he sent copies of the letter to a friend at the college where he had formerly taught, to one colleague in his present department, to an old classmate living in Canada (did Canada *have* trading stamps?), and to two former students—one in California and the other in Texas—neither of whom had heard from Tate in two or three years. He enclosed with each letter a brief hand-written note, promising to say more later.

Next he rummaged around in the pockets of his raincoat and found some twenty or thirty Green Stamps he had gotten the last time he bought gas. He counted out ten and put them in an envelope addressed to the people in Wisconsin. He stamped all six envelopes; on his way to class that afternoon, he mailed them.

His attitude toward the arrival of the mail changed somewhat. Refusals to like his poems disappointed him less than before; acceptances seemed not to mean so much. Morning after morning he went to the box for trading stamps, but morning after morning he came back with none.

"It said twenty-seven days," his wife would remind him.

"I know," he would snap, dropping seat-cover fabric samples into the kitchen wastebasket. He went downstairs and re-read the letter, which he had taped to the wall above his typewriter. He shuffled irritably through the student papers. He did hear from his friend in Canada and from his former colleague; both of them said they thought the voter bus was a good idea.

Now, instead of having a Martini before dinner and watching the cartoon shows, Tate made the children play in the basement and took to sitting soberly in front of the television news to watch for reports from the South. There were many—of shootings, explosions, foul-mouthed mothers. He cursed the news pictures out loud.

More than a month after he received the bus letter, an envelope with ten Prince Pig trading stamps showed up in his mailbox.

"Now it begins," he told his wife.

"I wonder who gives these," his wife said.

Two weeks later, ten more stamps arrived.

"Bonny Scot," Tate's wife read, peering at them and frowning. Tate shrugged. It was the cause, not the name of the stamps, that was important.

The following day came a letter with a Rhode Island postmark:

> Dear Mr. and Mrs. Morgan—
>   I have just received a chain letter suggesting that I send you 10 trading stamps (1¢ worth) on behalf of SNCC. If I followed this suggestion I should spend 30¢ in stamps for 1¢ mailed to SNCC. This seems a poor rate of return. Are you really going to sort out 10 stamps from each of the 3124 envelopes you are now receiving?
>   Would it not be better to send the equivalent 30 dollars to SNCC, as I have just done, and save the bother and cost? Commitment to a radical movement demands a seriousness beyond a 1920s gimmick of the kind you have initiated to reach the group of people that now includes myself.
>
>   Sincerely yours,
>   G. B. Hollis

The letter was hand-written on thin paper; the penmanship was masculine, but gracefully foreign-looking. Tate showed it to his wife, then carried it down to his study for further consideration.

He was disturbed, ruffled, because the letter seemed to make him stupid. He had never taken the trouble to do the mathematics of the plan, but his annoyance was over more than the loss of 576 envelopes from his mailbox. He fed paper into his typewriter and wrote a stiff answer:

> My dear Mr. Hollis,
>   I assume the chain-letter 'gimmick' in this case was initiated by someone in SNCC. At any rate, it wasn't any of my doing; like you, I became a part of it through tenuous interdependencies of friendships. It strikes me that continuing such a chain is something one does on the side, an action quite apart from whatever one is otherwise doing to further this particular movement—but I don't intend either to defend or deplore the gimmick. Whether anyone whose name rises to the top of the list really gets 3124 letters, or whether someone like you recoils from the silliness of it all and simply writes a check, the gimmick does work after a fashion, and (I trust) the bus for the voters gets bought.
>
>   Cordially yours,
>   T. Morgan

Tate read the letter over and underscored the words "quite apart from whatever one is otherwise doing," then showed it to his wife.

"What *are* you otherwise doing?" she said.

"At least I'm serious about the thing; I didn't break the damned chain," he said. He tucked the letter into its envelope, hunched on his coat, and left for the university.

During the next six weeks, covering a passage of time from autumn into winter, the batteries in the study radio slowly died. For the few days it took Tate to remember to buy new batteries, he read the student papers and fiddled with the small poems against a background of silence. Though he still might happen to be downstairs at mail time, he was able to invent new devices for checking on the arrival of the truck. He noticed beforehand if the neighbors had left their box-flags up, and looked out regularly to see if the postman had dropped the flags. If there had been rain or light snow, he squinted to discover tread marks close to the curbing. If the day was windless, he watched out for signs of lingering tremor in the thin pipe supporting the mailbox.

No more trading stamps found their way to the box. The children were allowed to come back to the television cartoons, the small poems went out and returned with the junk mail and the peculiar magazines. At first Tate was inclined to blame weak-link G. B. Hollis for stopping the flow to him of stamps, but by the end of the semester, when he put his twenty stamps into an envelope addressed to SNCC, he had come to realize how foolish the chain letter had been from the very beginning.

5. Proposing, 1975

THE young woman asks:
"What is the most beautiful thing you ever saw?"
"Your eyes, melting, when we first made love."
"You always tease me, lie to me."
"I'm only coaxing you to marry me."
"You have had one wife."
"Yes."
"I've had no husbands."
"So you once announced."
"And now you doubt me?"
"No. But I am older than you."
"And wiser?"
"And more suspicious."
"*Really* what is the most beautiful thing you ever saw?"
"Let me think."
"Oh, what nonsense."
"Why *nonsense?*"
"One doesn't *think* about beauty."

"An old man does."

"You're merely twice my age."

"But old enough to have to think hard about beauty."

"Because you must sort through so much of it?"

"Because it is so hard to remember what there is so little of."

"You're teasing me again."

"I'm trying to be serious."

The young woman smiles:

"Still, you *are* rather old."

"Yes."

"And these May-December . . . *liaisons* seldom last."

"Often they do. Think of the famous old men who have taken young wives: the statesmen, the artists . . ."

"But they are famous."

"Ah. What is the definition of *fame?*"

"And what is the definition of *age?*"

"My answer is: The most beautiful thing I ever saw was an old man with a young wife."

The man sighs:

"If I don't always answer your questions, it is because my parents raised me to be wary of them, therefore chary of answers. Don't mistake this for lack of wit. Don't either mistake it, or try to correct it."

The young woman looks perplexed:

"How does a man know when he has grown old?"

"He hears noises."

"Of?"

"In his head: of paper tearing. In his heart: of water freezing."

"And?"

"And he sees signs."

"In the eyes of others? In mirrors? In memories?"

"All of those. And in his children."
"They remind him?"
"They *become* him."
"They threaten him?"
"No. They are disinterested; oblivious."
"But he doesn't stop loving."
"Clearly he does not."
"He loves less forcibly?"
"He relaxes more. He gathers himself. He learns concentration. He takes naps on warm afternoons, and is careful not to dream."

The young woman sits before her mirror:
"What shall we do today?"
"What we did yesterday."
"Be plain."
"You know."
"Would I tell you I didn't if I did? Say what it is."
"It's something my generation wouldn't say."
"Wouldn't?"
"Didn't need to. We didn't need those words."
"Everything needs words."
"Not in my day."
"Then what did you use? Sign language? Morse code?"
"We knew. We simply *knew*."
"Telepathy? Intuition? I've no talent for that."
"We understood."
"I don't have second sight. Nor even, sometimes, *first* sight."
"Love at. . . ."
"You have to spell things out for me."
"We've never had much faith in words, my generation."
"How so."
"I think they were always too coarse for us—or too Latin."
"Vulgar, or vulgate. And so you lost faith."
"Something like that."

"What sort of *something?*"

"No. I'm sorry. I don't have words for it."

"And as for yesterday, I wonder sometimes if we do that too much."

The man smiles wryly:

"Words, you see, are self-indulgent."

"Oh, dear. How may a word indulge itself?"

"The users of words, I mean: the makers."

"Which?"

"Both. Users and makers."

"How do they indulge?"

"The makers: by claiming."

"And?"

"The users: by disclaiming."

"Am *I* not a word?"

"Your name is a word."

"And do you thereby claim me?"

"Yes."

"Then you are a maker."

"Sometimes."

"But if you had never known my name—"

"—Perhaps I could not have loved you."

"Then you would be a user."

"Why?"

"Because you would disclaim me."

"Never."

"Then you contradict yourself and your love is false."

"No. Real. That is *always* understood."

The man studies her:

"What do you want to be when you grow up?"

"Nothing."

"No ambitions?"

"None."

"You could be a wife."

"That would be embarrassing."

"Oh?"

"To be a wife is to be less than nothing."

"And?"

"Oh, to aspire to nothing, and possibly to fail at it—"

"The failure would embarrass you?"

"Would kill me."

"Ah."

"Death isn't *nothing*. Stop smirking."

"Forgive me."

"All right, I forgive."

The woman draws a long breath:

"But listen. If we begin to talk about love and death as if they were twins with the same last names, then we are hopeless romantics. And romance upsets me; it turns my stomach. Really listen. If I remember dying under you in the completion of an act of love, I'm only resorting to metaphor. You mustn't, merely because you are older, be *literal* with me. I am not killing you with tenderness. We do not actually explode together. The cannibalism we sometimes share is only fictitious. Oh, there is a profound difference between *history* and *love*. Don't ever dare tell me you would die for me; you have to die in spite of me."

"My generation—"

"Oh, God, I know: Would never need to say such things."

The man laughs:

"So you see what an indulgence they are."

"Words."

"Yes."

"No. Having spoken them, I don't feel any more satisfied."

"Marry me, then."

"Because by giving me a *new* name you may forever after indulge yourself in it?"

Now the man frowns:
"I have had one wife."
"Yes. Please, yes."
"She left me."
"I know. Please."
"You never asked me why."
"I thought she had died."
"She isn't dead. She inhabits my daughter."
"A miniature."
"Something like that."
"Something. She is my age, your daughter."
"Yes."
"Then will you have two wives?"
"Body and soul. Soul and body."
"More indulgence."
"*My* ambition has always been—"
"—To be contradictory?"
"—To be suspended between the living and the dead, and to turn unceasingly like a green planet."

The woman hesitates:
"I have to give you an answer."
"If you please."
"So. I will not marry your contradictions, nor will I be your child. But I will take naps with you on the warm afternoons forever."
"That is beauty enough."
"And I will remember everything except your birthdays."
"That is beauty more than enough."
"So you and I may become a ceremony of indulgences."
"Nothing more?"
"But nothing less."
"Do you promise?"
"I promise. I do. O yes."

Paint

SHE begins her weekend as usual—at the supermarket, letting her sons go off to play while she shops—but when she reaches the checkout counter things go shamefully wrong. The fault is her own, and yet at the moment when the girl at the cash register punches the last key and the total flickers into view in spidery red figures, she wishes deeply that she could blame someone, anyone, for the embarrassment that sweeps over her. She hasn't enough money. She has 35 dollars in her purse; the purchases add up to a little over 38. She has forgotten the checkbook.

"I'm awfully sorry," she says. "I have to put something back."

The girl, perhaps half her age, looks—what? Not angry; none of the clerks have that much commitment to the store, nor to their own work-time. Impatient. Condescending, perhaps—as if this high school girl with her long blonde hair drawn back into a ponytail, no gray in it, no color from a bottle, feels superior to a wife who has never learned to plan her shopping, to take into account the elastic food prices, to be—simply—prepared.

"I feel really stupid," she says to the girl. And knowing it is exactly the wrong thing to say, she looks down and begins fumbling with the cans and cartons under her hands. Some of the items she picked from the shelves are already gone, stuffed by a clumsy boy into double-thick kraft bags and laid into a wire cart

143

with a number dangling from the front of it. The rest lie before her in the circle of the counter's turntable, bunched against the rubber stop-bar. She rummages among cans and jars, looking at the violet price markings, increasingly conscious of people—perhaps a line—halted behind her.

"It happens, ma'am," the girl says. She tears off the register tape and searches under the stand for a pencil.

In the end she selects peanut butter, bacon, three packages of frozen vegetables, and pulls them away—bending to embrace them—from everything else.

"I'll put them back," she tells the girl.

"That's all right, ma'am. I'll get one of the stockboys." The girl bows her head over the register tape, subtracting. She pushes a lever at the side of the register; a door snaps open, and she scribbles inside with the pencil. A few coins slide into the round metal tray.

"Thank you," she says to the girl. She turns to the people stalled behind her. "I'm so sorry," she says. "Thank you for waiting."

At the car, rummaging in her purse for the key to unlock the door, the number tag held tightly in her teeth, she feels herself still blushing, sweat trickling under her arms, her knees weak. Once inside the car she rolls down all the windows to let out its heat; driving through the parking lot she cannot move fast enough to stir a breeze. At the supermarket entrance she pulls up the trunk lid—it no longer springs up of its own accord—and stands aside, the tag clutched in her hands while the stockboy sets the three brown paper bags—only three!—into the trunk. He closes the lid heavily ("That's the kind of slam-bang treatment that's wrecked the hinges," her husband would say), and takes the tag from her. She cannot tip him.

She wonders where the children have gotten to, and stands indecisively beside the car. Finally she sees them—Chris and Matthew—far up the line of stores, playing on a mechanical rocking horse in front of the Woolco. She waves, calls; when neither boy responds, she begins to feel foolish, as if she were calling home a dog or cat with a silly name. She gets into the car and drives slowly toward the Woolco to claim them.

When she pulls into the driveway her husband, Paul, is crouched on the back stoop, painting. The stoop is cement and has to be painted with a special mixture that will adhere and not flake away in the weather. The paint is vividly red, the color of first blood. She can see that he has already painted the front; the front is more porch-like, overhung by roof, but it, too, is cement. Now it glows scarlet in the waning sunlight. She waves as the car coasts to a stop. Paul lifts the brush toward her.

"You can't come in," he says.

She is half out of the front seat. "Why can't I?"

"Not dry," he says.

"Can't we just step over it?"

"No," he says. "I've painted the sills, too."

"Then can't we go in the front way?"

"I just got through painting there."

"Well, Paul—" She hears her voice breaking, frustrated.

"I'm sorry," he says. "I wanted to do it while I had the time and the urge."

She gets out of the car, leaving the door opened behind her. The two boys sit in unaccustomed silence in the back seat, watching and listening. She stands at the foot of the steps; the smell of the paint makes her head swim.

"Paul, really—" She puts her hands to her temples and draws them back through her hair.

"I think Mom has a headache," Christopher says softly.

"No, no. I'm trying to think." She lets her arms fall to her side. "Why don't you two go play until suppertime."

"Let's go to Hazen's," Matthew says.

"But don't leave the neighborhood," she calls after them. She sits on the car's front bumper and watches her husband slowly paint his way into the kitchen. He looks up.

"You oughtn't to sit there," he says. "That bumper support's pretty far gone with rust."

She stands and walks toward the back door. "Look," she says, "could I get you to take the meat down to the freezer? I don't want it to spoil."

"Just let me finish this," he says.

"Oh, for God's sake." She spins away from him and gets back into the car; it smells of heat, of musty leather, of old cigarette butts jammed into the ashtray tipped out above the dashboard clock. She half hopes to smell rotting hamburger. What is the matter with Paul? She puts her head out the window. "I'll be over at Marge Van Meter's," she tells him.

"What would I do without your freezer compartment?" she says. She has driven the three blocks to Marge's house in a kind of anger that is close to rage—a depth of emotion she realizes she rarely feels. The ground meat is safely tucked away in the top of the Van Meter refrigerator; a pound of margarine and a package of sliced cheese sit on one of the shelves below. Marge is a close friend. The two women borrow from each other, depend on each other for small favors, complain to each other. She has told Marge about Paul's behavior, and now—Marge listens so placidly—she feels nearly calm.

"It's ridiculous," Marge says. She puts down two coffee cups and brings the carafe from the stovetop. "It's really killing."

She sips at the coffee; her hands, she notices, are trembling. "But they've needed paint—those porchy places," she says. "I should be grateful."

Marge is studying her. "How are things going at home? I mean other than painting-wise."

"Fine." She wonders if Marge finds this odd paint episode to be the symptom of something deep. "Are Paul and I topics?"

Marge looks sheepish. "Heavens, no," she says.

"I think I'll phone."

She lets the phone ring a half-dozen times, then breaks the

connection and re-dials her number. This time the phone rings ten times before she hangs up.

"He's probably in the cellar, cleaning brushes," she says.

"Probably."

She sits at the formica table, turning the half-empty cup in its saucer. "I should check on the boys."

"Where are they?"

"I think over at Hazen Donnelly's."

"They're all right. Penny keeps an ear open."

She says nothing. The scene she has left at home revolves in her mind—Paul forcing her away from her own door, making her wait; how angry she is, and at the same time baffled.

"I think I'll drive over home," she says.

"There's more coffee."

"No, thanks. I'll call you—or come back if there's a problem." But how could there be a problem?

When she arrives, Paul is nowhere to be seen. Both the front and back doors are open; the curtains at the window of the dining area blow lazily in the small wind passing through the house. The afternoon sun, reflected off the shiny red surface of the back steps and doorsill, is like a stack of lacquered chinese boxes.

She approaches the back door with an extraordinary caution. She does not touch the painted cement to see if it has dried, but halts uncertainly at the end of the walk. She can see inside the kitchen the doorway to the cellar and beside it the handle of the refrigerator door; a few newspapers are spread over the carpet, and drops of scarlet paint are spattered on them.

"Paul?" The name catches in her throat, like a word she has not pronounced in a long time. She repeats it, and listens. No answer. The cellar light is off; perhaps he is at the back of the house.

She walks into the back yard and threads her way through rosebushes until she stands at their bedroom window. The sun glares back at her; she puts her hand against the glass and peers in under its shadow. Paul is not there—apparently. He might (she thinks stupidly) be hiding from her, might be flattened against the wall beside the window—but why would he do that? She continues around the end of the house until she is between the two junipers under the window of the boys' room. This room, too, is empty. She finishes her circuit of the house, arrives at the front door—and here she encounters Paul, standing just inside the doorway, watching her narrowly.

"What the hell are you doing?" he says. "Inspecting the place?"

"I was trying to find you."

"Here I am."

"When can I come in?"

"When the paint dries."

"And when will that be?"

"Overnight, at least."

She stares at him.

"I think we should follow the directions," he says.

"Are you truly going to keep me out of my own house until tomorrow?"

"It looks that way."

"And the boys?"

"I guess."

She tries to make sense of this. "What's the matter with you?" she says. "What are you up to?"

"Nothing. Nothing's the matter with me."

"My God, I can't believe you're doing this." She clenches her fists, as if she might, instead of only glaring at her husband, go stamping up the front steps and pummel him. She thinks of doing just that. But when she imagines the soles of her shoes sticking on the wet paint, the effort of lifting her feet out of the red, tacky surface, the sound like paper tearing of her shoes breaking contact—she puts the idea out of her mind.

"It is," he says. "Happening."

She tries to stare him down, make his eyes turn away from hers, but his gaze is steady as can be; it is her own eyes that look elsewhere—down at his hands, which hang at his sides, the fingers stained red, though now the color is faded from scrubbing.

"I don't know what to do," she says. The dizziness has returned; it is as if she has had too much to drink—or perhaps as if she has not slept for a long time, and giddiness has taken hold of her.

"Whatever you want." He turns away from her, vanishes inside the house she has always shared with him. For an instant she thinks she will call him back, but something in a far corner of her mind tells her she must not beg him for anything.

Throughout, she has tried to think clearly, to be calm, to carry out precisely the actions of this odd life—as if what has to be done is a matter of calculation, like the electronic circuitry of the cash register at the supermarket. There is no use in giving way to the frustration she feels; certainly there is no arguing— threatening or weeping or coaxing—with Paul. The paint is wet; she must not step in it or over it; Paul will not permit her to enter her own kitchen, her own front hall. For a hysterical moment she has weighed the notion of climbing in through a bedroom window, but even if she can get the screen off from the outside, then what? She imagines Paul preventing her—painting the windowsills, possibly, or simply pushing her back, so that she hangs, half inside, half outside, for the neighbors to marvel at. ("Did you see Paul's wife trying to crawl in through their bedroom window?" "Oh, yes—nice legs, I thought.") She even considers calling the police—but they would hesitate to interfere in a domestic matter.

She chooses to spend the night at a motel—a Holiday Inn on the outskirts of town near the interstate. She has arranged for the boys to stay overnight at the Donnelly house, she has rejected—politely—Marge Van Meter's offer of her guest room ("I

don't want people to think of this as some sort of trial separa-
tion," she tells Marge.), she has made sure the American Ex-
press card is in her billfold so she will avoid any new version of
her earlier humiliation at the supermarket.

Despite such preparations, she feels awkward at the motel.
She has no luggage, and she thinks for a frantic instant of letting
herself be seen with an armful of the groceries she still carries in
the trunk of the car. When she signs the register, the appear-
ance of her name is almost foreign to her; she writes "Mrs. . . .",
then scratches it out. Should she have used her maiden name?
And should she invent an address? She decides to falsify nothing, then wonders what the clerk—another blonde, possibly a
sister of the cashier at the market—will think of a woman who
does not know if she is married, checking alone into a local
motel. Will her room be watched? Will her license plate be
phoned in to the police station for comparison with stolen car
lists? Will there, at some impossible early morning hour, be a
knock at the door of her room, someone for her to keep out?

The room itself is ordinary, filled with plastic surfaces and
corners, the wallpaper behind and above the pair of beds pretending to be a hazy view of a mountain lake through evergreen
branches that look to her to be oriental. This is another country,
say the furnishings, the mural, the ugly modern table lamp
which is lighted and casts a halo around the opened Bible. No
one lives here but you, say the mirrors above the dresser and
the oval sink beyond folding doors. The television set so domi-
nates one end of the room, she thinks it will talk to her whether
she turns it on or not.

Now that she is here, she has no idea what to do. The hour is
too early—it is barely dusk outside—for her to sleep; she has no
settling in to do, nothing to unpack or hang up. If she wants to
go out, she has no clothes to change into. When she does switch
on the television she finds a baseball game on the one channel
that comes in clearly; the others are in a murkiness of false color
that blurs edges and makes echoes out of people's features. She

turns the set off. The room is too warm, she notices, and she fiddles with the broken knob of the air-conditioner beside the one long window. Finally she takes off her blouse and washes her face and hands and arms at the exposed sink. What she looks like in the mirror under the fluorescent light is a woman in a foreign movie.

She feels better after she has washed—more composed, more in command of herself. She thinks about phoning Marge to say that she has checked in and to make fun of the surroundings. She thinks about phoning the Donnellys' to talk to Chris or Matthew. She even thinks about phoning Paul—but she is afraid to lose her temper and say something regrettable.

She wonders if she should treat herself to a drink; she can sign for it at the motel bar, and perhaps the alcohol will complete the task of relaxing her. She puts on the blouse—it feels cool; it feels like a different blouse from the one she has worn all day—and adjusts it at the waist, taking such great care that she persuades herself she is dressing up. In her purse she finds a comb and runs it through her hair. She freshens her lipstick. If she is not exactly a new woman, at least she is ready for a drink after a trying day.

But the bar disappoints her. It is dark, smells musty, is full of the loud voices of middle-aged men. When she sits at the bar, one of the men appears next to her and offers to buy her a drink. She thanks him, but declines. Later, while she is sipping a second martini, the same man returns. He is balding, has plump cheeks, looks at her with watery eyes she thinks may be gray. He talks to her; she scarcely listens until all at once she realizes he is asking her to his room, that his voice has fallen to a lower volume and one of his eyebrows is arched. When he stops talking, she tries to find words for an answer; instead, she begins to laugh. She is embarrassed to realize that she cannot stop laughing, that she has the kind of uncontrollable giggles she used to have when she was at summer camp with other young girls, talking after dark about boys.

When she wakes up light is bursting into the room over the top of the drapes and through the crack of window alongside the door of the room. She holds up her left arm, maneuvering her wrist until the watch catches the sliver of brightness and she can read seven o'clock. Paul will not be awake yet. Nor will the boys at the Donnellys'. It is Sunday morning. In a motel she always expects to be torn from sleep by the sound of the maids' carts rumbling along concrete balconies, but there is none of that this morning and she wonders what waked her. The only noise is the air-conditioning unit under the window. What should she do? Perhaps if she dresses and goes to the coffee shop she will meet the man from the bar, and begin laughing again.

She rolls over and sprawls face down in the soft bed. This is the first time in her married life she has deliberately slept alone. It is unpleasant—like a punishment, all the more unfair because self-imposed. It suggests that she has waked up not from mere sleep, but from her connections with Paul, with their sons, with old neighbors—and that she has entered into a new sort of consciousness whose relationships are fragile and must be labored at. She wonders if it is too early to go home—if the drying time is up so the paint can be walked on. Now that she is rested, she understands that she has to force herself out of this—what? Out of this acquiescence, this narrow dependence on the customary arrangements of life.

She dresses quickly, tries to polish the surfaces of her teeth with a forefinger wet under the cold water tap, makes a few passes—habit—at the coverlet of the bed. Inside her purse she discovers a half-used roll of mint candy; she pops one wafer into her mouth. Before she leaves the room behind—forever, she imagines—she looks around carefully, as if she had actually brought anything to mislay.

Arriving at home she sees that both the front and back doors are closed, both sets of steps glossy—like liquid—in morning sun. Before she goes up the back steps she touches them, gin-